Subarbis

A PLAY

Timothy Harsh

**Outskirts Press, Inc.
Denver, Colorado**

This is a work of fiction. The events and characters described herein are imaginary and are not intended to refer to specific places or living persons. The opinions expressed in this manuscript are solely the opinions of the author and do not represent the opinions or thoughts of the publisher. The author has represented and warranted full ownership and/or legal right to publish all the materials in this book.

Subarbis
All Rights Reserved.
Copyright © 2010 Timothy J. Harsh
v2.0 r1.0

The image for the cover is a reproduction of an original painting by Neil Driver
http://neildriver.com/

This book may not be reproduced, transmitted, or stored in whole or in part by any means, including graphic, electronic, or mechanical without the express written consent of the publisher except in the case of brief quotations embodied in critical articles and reviews.

Outskirts Press, Inc.
http://www.outskirtspress.com

ISBN: 978-1-4327-4830-2

Outskirts Press and the "OP" logo are trademarks belonging to Outskirts Press, Inc.

PRINTED IN THE UNITED STATES OF AMERICA

The Characters

Art…………..mid forties

Sara………...late forties

Kelly………...seventeen

Frank………..eighteen

Lisa…………..nineteen

Brad………....nineteen

Patterson…....mid sixties

The Man……mid forties

The Setting

Suburbia in America.
Present day.

Battle of the Breast

Friday Night, 7:30 PM

A kitchen in middle-class suburban America. We're afforded all the luxuries of such a time and place: an oversized stainless steel refrigerator, a large butcher block island around which most activity revolves, numerous pots and pans hanging above the island, canisters of imported coffee beans on the counter. The glasses and dinnerware are various matching shades of dark blue. There is a discarded soccer ball on the floor next to a dirty soccer jersey and a pair of running shoes. A few feet away, there is a backpack on the floor with an open textbook and a notebook carelessly on top of it.

There is an open door stage right that leads to the unseen backyard grill area and an archway off the kitchen that leads to a dining room. There is also a staircase leading directly into this kitchen from the second floor.

Art and Sara are preparing a meal. They cross each

other, each tending to different chores, and there is silence. There seems to be no animosity, simply silence for the lack of much to say. Art walks to the refrigerator as Sara turns, their paths intersecting -- a slight hesitation before they both adjust their paths and continue.

The silence continues for an extended moment until...

Art: I'm not so sure this dinner was the greatest idea.

Sara: Why.

Art: It's embarrassing.

Sara: Embarrassing?

Art: Well no, but it's like saying look at me, is all.

Sara: We're not throwing a *gala*, Art -- good Lord.

Art: Maybe embarrassing's the wrong word. I appreciate it, I really do.

Sara: I would hope so. This will be your third book; you deserve something.

Art: You're right … I just … the dinner should be about everyone getting together to eat and drink, you know -- not celebrating. I hate being the center.

Sara: Well, Art, if you don't want to be the center don't be the center. Just cook the food and laugh when someone says something funny.

Art: That's all there is to it?

Sara: Not much to ask.

Art: But thanks for putting this all together and inviting Patterson. I wouldn't have thought of it. I just wouldn't. You're a sweetheart.

He leans in to kiss her on the cheek but as he does this Sara unknowingly turns and leans the other way, reaching for the wine bottle.

Sara: The bathroom ceiling has mold on it.

Art: I know -- we need to do something.

Sara: Well...

Art: Well...we can...rub it out.

She cocks her head, looks at him.

Sara: *Rub* it out?

Art: *Yes*. Rub it out.

Sara: No, not with mold -- you don't want to touch it, you just paint over it and let just the brush touch it, I think. Never touch it. It needs it anyway --

Art: But that doesn't really *solve* the mold. (*Then*) Did you see the paper? It was interesting the other day --

Sara: Who says you have to *solve* it? It's fungus, I think. Spores of it. If you go in there upsetting it, the spores'll be embedded in your lungs, first day. God, as if the world isn't bad enough, your own *house* is a battle zone. (*Then*) What was that color --

Art: --they said the universe is actually shaped exactly like the earth...round.

Sara: --it's *Sandstone,* is that what the Richardsons did with their hallway? I like that color.

Art: Actually spherical, I guess, would be more accurate. But doesn't the *idea* of a sphere denote an edge? I mean, if they're really saying sphere, there's an edge, right? Amazing stuff, it really is. To think we're all moving at mind-boggling speeds through a sphere. I think I should maybe sit in on some of the astronomy classes at the University -- wonder if I should have gone into that, I would have been good. (*Looking around*) Where's that goddamned paper? (*Yelling upstairs*) Frank! Where's the paper!

Sara: It *was* Sandstone. Let's get that next weekend, let's just do it with some white trim. I'll even do it, you don't have to.

He moves a magazine aside, searching for the paper. Unsuccessful, he drops his shoulders, exhales.

Art: Just want that article, I mean it's a pretty simple request, just want five minutes to read an article, have you seen it? It also has the front story, comparing American supremacy to the Roman Empire, but not what you'd expect, and should American supremacy continue in the next hundred years, as in, is it best for the world? Great paper, really is, best thirty bucks I've spent all year, especially if I could actually read it.

Sara: (*Grabbing bowls from the cupboard*) Why don't you just read it online?

Art: Because I want something in my *hands* -- I want to feel like I'm getting something for my thirty bucks, and who in their right mind stares at a computer screen for an hour, reading?

Sara: Lots of people, so if you don't want to help with the bathroom next weekend I'm actually happy doing it myself -- for alone time, I mean.

Art: I mean really, is that where we're all headed? Does *everything* have to be digital? No one's going to have sight anymore from staring at screens twenty-four hours a day. I will, though --

Sara: Remember when we painted the bathroom in my apartment in college?

Art: --because I'm not threatened by staying with paper. (*Then*). Which apartment?

Sara: We went to *Berkeley*, remember, Art?

Art: I just...what apartment, again?

Sara: The one on Telegraph.

Art: Hmmm.

Sara: Third time we had sex.

Art: I remember.

She looks at him.

Sara: We were standing up.

Art: I said I remember.

Sara: And the neighbor was watching.

Art begins cutting a loaf of bread.

Art: Seems like so long ago.

Sara: Now if our neighbors watched I'd be *mortified*...Lord, could you imagine? Could never have another dinner party.

Art: (*Staring at the bread*) Maybe we should live in a place where the neighbors *could* watch.

She rubs a bit of sweat from her forehead.

Sara: We haven't had sex in the bathroom of *this* house.

Art: I think we have.

Sara: We've been here for twenty years.

He stops slicing.

Art: Has it been…

Sara: Did you hear me?

Nothing.

Sara: Well, I'm not in the business of scheduling bathroom sex with my own husband -- I mean, don't you think that's one thing that *shouldn't* be scheduled in life? (*Then*) When's Patterson supposed to get here? I want to have these appetizers timed.

Art places a mushroom in the middle of the cutting board. He takes the knife between his thumb and index finger, raises it high above his head and releases it. The knife falls, sticking in the cutting board - missing its target.

Sara watches this then takes a drink of wine. He places his left hand on the cutting board, spreading his fingers wide apart then lifts the knife with his other hand.

His eyes slowly look over to Sara.

She shrugs her shoulders. His eyes shift back to focus on his hand. He releases the knife.

Voice (O.S.): Daddy!!

He flinches and pulls his hand away at the last second — the knife sticks in the board.

Sara: Too bad.

Kelly trots down the stairs and approaches the island.

Kelly: Daddy, I think I need a glass of wine, since it's a special occasion, you know?

She's wearing a small, thin white tank top and jeans. The jeans ride so low the top of her underwear is visible riding her narrow hips. She sits on one of the stools lining the island.

They stop what they are doing and stare at her...

Kelly: It's not like Dad gets published everyday. Think I'd like some red, maybe what you're having, Sara.

Still silence.

Kelly: *What.*

Sara: I think you know what.

Kelly: I think I don't.

Sara: You need to go up stairs and put on a bra. That tank top is like a napkin.

She looks at her chest.

Kelly: What…

Art: Honey, you can see right through it.

Sara: It's unacceptable.

Kelly reaches for a clean wine glass.

Kelly: Don't be ashamed of my body.

Sara: You know it's not that, but some things are respectable and some things aren't, especially when we have company coming over.

Kelly: Who's coming over?

Art: Patterson.

Kelly: Oh…Who else.

Art: Just Patterson, it's not a *gala*.

Kelly: Well, if it's just Patterson, he's almost like family -- I mean, he's been your editor for like twenty years … who's he to care?

Art: But he's also head of the philosophy department at the University and my boss…so *please.*

She stands up and places her hands on her breasts.

Kelly: What's with the interrogation, I mean, how about a "Hi, honey, good to see you!" or "How's my little muffin today, my sweet little baby girl, my only daughter" … all that crap?

Sara: Please, enough with the drama, Kelly -- I need to get this dinner ready and I could use some help, so spare us.

Kelly: Fine, but does it strike you odd that the first thing that entered your mind when I sat down was my breasts?

A long beat…

Art: Whom are you asking?

Kelly points with both of her hands, one finger at each of them, and then in the same motion drops her right hand and reaches for the wine bottle.

Sara: You aren't having wine.

Kelly: You're skirting the question, I'm asking both of you: Why are my breasts the center of attention?

Sara: They're not the center of attention; it's simply about respect — there are *rules* in society.

Kelly: I'm not *in* society, I'm in my own *house* and apparently my own family has issues with my body. Why does it make you uncomfortable that you can see my breasts? That's all I'm asking, and the very thought of having to answer that is as troubling to you as having to see my nipples.

Sara: It's not your breasts - -

Kelly: *Nipples.* If you can't even say it, mother …

Sara: -- it's the fact that your dress is just not acceptable for tonight.

Kelly: What's the difference? You're talking in circles and you know that doesn't work with me because I'm too smart. I got Daddy's brain --

Kelly fills her glass with wine.

Kelly: --no offense, Mom, I got your sense of adventure, which is fine, like how you wanted to live abroad when you graduated --

Art: Honey, you shouldn't be drinking wine, you're seventeen.

Kelly: --even though you ended up not doing it isn't the point, it's that it's in your nature to at least *want* to, to have that drive. I think I got that. Like how I *really* can't wait to get out of this house after I graduate next year. Lucky Frank -- that bastard gets to leave this year if he ever stops masturbating long enough to open an acceptance letter.

Sara: Don't talk about Frank like that.

Art: Speaking of, where is he?

Kelly: Upstairs.

Art: Well, I could use some help with the grill, would you go up and see if he can come down.

Kelly: I'd rather not, if that's ok.

Art: *(Cocks his head)* Please…

Kelly: *Fine.*

She gets up, takes her glass of wine with her and starts for the stairs.

Sara: And put a bra on! Patterson will be here any minute.

Kelly exits.

Art pulls a container of chicken breasts from the refrigerator and begins prepping them.

Sara: Can we get that soccer ball and that jersey out of here? It's been there all day -- and that backpack. I mean, is anyone *really* studying in this house?

Art: We'll have Frank do it.

Sara: It's right *there.*

Art: I have chicken on my hands.

Sara: Impossible to keep this place clean, I swear, Patterson'll think we live like this all the time.

Art: We *do…*

Sara: (*Raises a huge knife*) *No*, we don't.

He steps back.

Art: Nothing to be ashamed of.

Sara: We live decent lives, Art, we don't live in filth. There's a difference between messy and *dirty.*

Art regards this for a moment before wiping his hands on a towel. He takes a bottle of J&B on the counter and pours himself half a glass. Sara grabs a handful of ice cubes from the nearby ice bin and places them in his drink.

Art: Thought I'd have this one without ice.

Sara: It's no fun without ice.

He looks at her for a moment, then drinks from his glass. He exhales, looks at the ice cubes.

Sara: We really need to talk about Kelly.

Art: What about her?

Sara: She's become so disrespectful.

Art: She's just challenging ideas … she's fine.

Sara: (*Lifts the knife*) You can *challenge* ideas; just do it with a bra on. How will her ideas ever get respect when her breasts are the center of attention?

Art: You kind of made them the center of attention, Sara.

Sara: It's about respect for your family, with no bra at dinner, I never did that. It's just to probe us.

Art: She's always needed a lot of attention. We have to allow her to have that. (*Then*) And maybe she has some points.

Sara: What?

Art: It *is* just the human body, if you really look at it that way, she maybe has a point. I mean, why was it that we made her feel like she did something wrong? When you look at it as parents, what's worse — nipples, or drinking?

Sara: Nicely put, Art.

Art: Well…

Sara: I told her not to drink that five times. I think

you should have pulled it away from her.

Art: Wrestle her to the floor, maybe? Throw the glass against the wall? At least she's not drinking with the football team in a Mustang going seventy —

Sara: She did that?

Art: -- and the necking …

Sara: If I ever find out she's been doing that, it's really over.

Art: … and a DUI would be getting off easy with all the car accidents.

Sara: Oh God! Don't say that. Did she really do that?

Art: I don't know…no…I was just saying, you know, compared to having a glass of wine here in the kitchen, it doesn't look so bad.

Sara: It would be nice if I felt we were on the same side when it comes to the kids.

Art: We are.

Sara: Well, it doesn't feel like it sometimes.

She exhales.

Sara: It's exhausting…*I'm* exhausted. I'm sorry.

She wipes her hands, walks to him and kisses him on the forehead.

Art: (*Looks about the kitchen*) How can *this* be so tiring?

Sara: Would you please get that grill started? It takes an hour for it to just heat up. You've got to prep it.

Art: Doesn't take an *hour.*

Sara: Yes, it does. An hour. Where's Frank? Could he spend *any* more time in his room? I mean what did we do to raise a recluse?

He looks at her from the corner of his eye.

Sara: Don't answer that.

And with that Frank comes down the stairs and walks to the island. He looks like he's been sleeping, hair ruffled, baggy jeans, a wrinkled t-shirt.

A newspaper is rolled up and stuffed into his back pocket — this catches Art's attention as he quickly cranes his neck, looking at Frank's pocket. Art drops his knife.

Art: What the hell is that!

Art rushes him.

Sara: Hi, honey. What, are you sleeping all day now?

Frank comes to attention and raises his arms slightly in front of him — a meager attempt at self-defense.

Frank: (*Still in sleepy haze*) What's the *matter* with you?

Art lunges around to Frank's back pocket causing Frank to spin away from him, keeping it out of his reach.

Art: Stop moving!

Frank: (*Swatting at Art's hands*) What are you *doing*?

Art: I want my paper!

He lunges for it again. Frank stumbles back.

Sara: Art! Would you stop it? Just *ask* him for the paper.

Art: I paid for it.

Frank: I don't have your paper.

Art puts him in a headlock with one hand and reaches for the paper with the other.

Sara: Art! Stop it!

She throws a red pepper at him -- it hits him in the back and thuds to the floor.

Art: You do. You took it last week too.

Frank: The fuck I do.

And with that, Art snatches the paper, releases the headlock, and quickly walks behind the island, unrolling it.

Frank gathers himself, rubbing his neck...

Frank: Jesus....

...and sits at the island.

Sara: (*To Art*) What is the *matter* with you? (*Then to Frank*) Honey, are you ok? I'm sorry, your father has lost his mind.

Art looks at the front page, slaps it, then looks up.

Art: This is my paper.

Frank: You weren't reading it.

Art: How can I read it if you have it?

Frank: It was in a rubber band for three days.

Sara: Art, apologize to your son, please.

Art walks to Frank and places his hands on his shoulders.

Art: You're right, got a little excited. Frankie boy, I'm sorry, ok? Just got a little excited about this round universe article, pretty exciting stuff. (*Looks at Sara*) Can't have any fun anymore.

Frank: I read that, covers the Unified Theory too.

Art: (*To Sara*) Hear that? See, this is big stuff, Sara, important stuff.

He walks back around the island, energized. Sara and Frank watch him.

He folds the paper neatly and places it methodically on the exact corner of the island.

Art: Going to put this here and we're all good. For later.

Frank: Got that at a ninety-degree angle?

Art: Going to finish up this baby probably later on tonight. The universe article.

Sara: Oh, *which* article again? Glad you mentioned that one more time, I was going to ask you again why you wanted the paper…

Art: With the sarcasm around here, where do you think Kelly's getting it? (*Then to Frank*) Did any letters come yesterday?

Frank: No.

Sara: Well, I still want us to keep talking about Berkeley or Stanford. They're such great schools, Frank -- they just are.

Frank: I want to go to NYU. Berkeley's a bunch of burners.

Art: And pacifists.

Sara: Art...

Frank pours himself a glass of wine.

Frank: If I get accepted, the letter should come any day. It's all I really want, I'm telling you.

Sara: You should have a soda instead.

Frank: You shouldn't be buying soda -- it's terrible for you; not to mention Kelly drinks about five cans a day. Do we really think she needs more sugar? I mean, come on. (*Takes a drink of wine.*)

Sara: I just don't know why you can't be more open to going to school closer to home.

Frank: I want to live in New York. It's not fair to try to keep me here. Remember how it felt when you wanted to go overseas after you graduated?

Sara considers this...

Frank: Thank you. Just always try to remember that feeling, and we'll be on the same page.

Art: He's got a point.

Sara: It just seems like it's about getting away from us, more than NYU.

Frank: Well, it's that too.

Sara takes her glass of wine and walks around the island, puts her arm around Frank and kisses him on the cheek.

Sara: You don't mean that.

Frank: I actually do -- but isn't that what your children do? I mean, do you really expect me to stay around here through my college years? That's not what you want for me. I'd go fucking crazy and you know it —

He runs his hand through his already moppy hair; it's sticking everywhere.

Frank: I love you both, but you're both insane in that subtle kind of normal way which is probably the scariest form of insane. No offense, and none of your friends probably tell you that, because adults don't say what they mean.

Sara: So crucify me for wanting my children in my life. I just can't bear to think of this house with you gone.

Frank: So is it about wanting me here, or not wanting to face a really empty, really clean house?

She walks to the other side of the island.

And with this Kelly comes back down the stairs. She's wearing the exact same outfit as before.

Sara: (*To Frank*) It's *not* about an empty house.

Frank pays no attention to Kelly as he grabs food from the counter, eating.

Frank: Well, maybe when we're gone, you should consider selling this house and moving out of this neighborhood. I mean, the same neighbors, the same lawns, the years piling up....makes you think of dying. It does me, at least, and I'm not even in college yet.

Kelly sits next to Frank on the island stool.

Sara turns and sees Kelly.

Sara: (*Waves the knife*) *That's enough.* I'm serious this time. You will not live in this household and eat *our* food and drink *our* wine. What is the matter with you?

Kelly: *What?*

Frank: Who are you talking to?

Art: Just put on a different shirt.

Kelly: I had nothing clean to put on. I'm sorry, I tried, I really did. That's why I was gone so long. I have absolutely nothing to wear.

Frank slowly turns his head and looks at his sister's chest.

Sara: You will go up right now and put on a bra.

Frank stares, takes a drink of wine.

Sara: Frank! Stop!

Frank: What?

Sara: What do you mean *what*…(*Then*) Now this is making me a bit uncomfortable. There, I said it.

Kelly: Well, thanks for finally being honest. Maybe you're projecting your own issues with your body onto me. Maybe you just don't feel comfortable with parts of your body, which is completely normal when women reach their fifties.

Sara: *Forty-nine!*

Frank looks at her chest again.

Kelly: (*To Frank*) Wanna take a picture?

Frank: Who needs to, with that shirt?

Frank gets up and walks to the refrigerator.

Art: Look Kelly, let's just not make problems tonight with the dinner -- and can you all please play nice? Patterson's my *boss*...

Kelly: I'd really be happy to, but like I said, I don't have a clean bra, I just don't.

Frank walks back to the stool and notices the top of Kelly's underwear. He takes his index finger, gently hooks the elastic band and pulls it up. Art and Sara cannot see this. He takes his seat but his finger is still locked into her underwear.

Kelly stops mid-sentence and cocks her head. She looks at Frank, although he's looking straight at Art and Sara.

Sara: I don't want to talk about it anymore. Just go up and change. Put on a different shirt, sports bra, something.

Kelly: Ok, fine...If we're not going to drop this, fine...all we do is go in circles.

She reaches around her back and takes Frank's hand, trying to pry it from her underwear. It doesn't work.

Sara: You're taking years off my life -- is that what you want for me?

Kelly: Since you supply the wine, I guess not.

Kelly struggles with Frank's hand. She squirms, but he simply pulls her underwear further up and out of her jeans.

Kelly jerks forward.

Sara: What are you two doing? Please…

Kelly: Frank's wedging me.

Sara: Well, don't.

And with this Kelly takes her other hand and rams it into Frank's crotch, grabbing a handful.

Frank: Aghhh!

He releases her and grabs her arm; she doesn't release.

Art: Can you guys relax for five minutes? Frank, I think the chicken is ready -- let's get this grill going. It takes about an hour to prep.

Frank: (*In pain*) Doesn't take an *hour*.

Kelly continues to hold his crotch although she doesn't look at him. Frank holds her arm with both arms, trying to maintain some control.

Kelly: That's a good idea -- why don't you two get that baby going, and I'll —

Sara: *You'll* go up and change.

Kelly: That's what I was going to say.

She releases Frank's crotch; he exhales in relief. She looks at him and places her hand on the back of his head and leans in toward him.

Kelly: What's wrong, Frank? You seem a little jumpy.

Frank: Dad, can you throw me that rag, the wet one? There's some wine on the counter.

Art tosses him the rag. Frank grabs it and pushes it on Kelly's breast, soaking the thin tank top and rendering the breast fully visible.

Sara: Jesus.

Kelly: You're such a perv. Mom, you've raised a pervert -- I hope you're happy.

She turns to walk towards the stairway.

Art: So much for a normal dinner.

Kelly: (*Yelling*) Ok, Sara! Everyone take notice, I'm

going up- - stairs - - to - - change!

She walks up the first two stairs and with that the doorbell rings. Without missing a beat, she spins back around and heads for the door.

Kelly: I'll get it, mommy!

Sara: No!

She drops the knife and runs for the door -- knocking her glass of red wine all over the....

Art: My fucking paper!

He lunges for the glass but it's too late — wine splatters like a crime scene.

Frank grins and pours himself another glass.

Kelly reaches the door and opens it to reveal Patterson, who's wearing a dinner suit, bow tie, and black-rimmed glasses. He's holding a bottle of wine.

His pleasant smile quickly fades as his eyes drop to Kelly's chest.

She reaches both hands above her head and puts her hair into a momentary ponytail then lets it fall to her shoulders. She cocks her head.

Kelly: Hi, Patterson.

His mouth opens slightly but manages no words. She reaches to him…

Kelly: Let me take that wine for you.

Lights fade.

Relativity

Saturday, 9:15 AM

The Kitchen. Art and Brad sit at the table. Papers and books are spread before them, as is a pot of coffee. Brad holds a pen and writes notes on the paper in front of him throughout this exchange.

Art: I can give my students guidance, that's it. I can't *write* it for you. I'm not a crutch here…

Art gets up and begins pacing.

Brad: I understand that, I'm not asking you to.

Art: Let's take a look at page five, third paragraph down. You touch on one of the distinct elements of twentieth century realism that there is a commonsense belief that physical objects like the sun or the stars exist independently of the mind…this is your belief.

Brad: Yes, I guess.

Art: You guess.

Brad: Yes, it is.

Art stops and looks at him before beginning to walk around the table, circling him.

Art: Do you *believe* it…or is it for the purpose of generating a thesis?

Brad: No, I believe it as well.

Art: Ok…can you prove it?

Brad: Prove what?

Art: That something you cannot hear or see exists?

Brad: Yes.

Art: How?

Brad: Ahh…

Art: Ok, let's see … your mother. She lives on the coast.

Brad: Yes.

Art: How do you know she exists at this immediate point in time?

Brad: (*He hesitates*) I *know* she is alive, she *exists*.

Art: You believe it.

Brad: I know it.

Art: You *know* it, precisely, so if you were to call her right now, she would talk to you. You would hear her, you could communicate to her.

Brad: Exactly. Proven.

Art: Proven to you. What are those things?

Brad: What?

Art: Things like her voice.

Brad: Not sure what you're getting at.

He walks closer to Brad and kneels beside him.

Art: Let me put it this way….We're made of muscle, bone, neurons, brain matter, soft tissue. Our sense of the physical world is only a sensory representation produced by our input systems, symbols whose only meaning is derived from what is learned -- a car, a block of wood, a blue sky…a mother. Why do you associate one emotion to a block of wood and another emotion to your mother?

Brad: Sound like your lectures.

Art: These "emotions" are chemical reactions in your brain mass housed in your skull. That's it….So, your mother exists….All of this around you *exists,* according to you.

He stands again and begins walking around the table.

Art: "Exists" is a relative term. Is what I'm getting at. For something to exist it must be seen by an eye, heard by an ear, touched by a finger -- a signal must be sent to the mass of neurons which is your brain, and a chemical reaction must take place for us to understand it and label it as "existing." All other is technically a "belief,"-- "faith," as it's sometimes called. Do you agree?

Brad: (*Hesitates, thinking*) Yes.

Art: Ok, based on that understanding of the definition, would your mother "exist" if you were not alive? If you were dead. If you were cremated and your brain, your eyes, your neurons were not functioning, if they were turned to ash, put in a 3 by 3 box and someone threw dirt over them while bawling their eyes out.

Brad: Well, yes. She still would.

Art runs over to him quickly.

Art: By whose definition! In what realm!? (*He begins laughing*) Certainly not yours!

Brad: In the realm of only those who are still alive, whose brains can process her existence.

Art: So she can both exist *and* not exist at the same time.

Brad: I guess so…

Art: You guess so…Existence is relative then, is what you're saying -- not absolute.

Brad: Yes…relative to the observer.

Art: (*Slowly*) Relative to the observer…yes… (*Then*) There are no absolute values in life Brad; unfortunately life is not a calculus equation.

Art stops and exhales. He walks slowly behind him and places both hands on Brad's shoulders, rubbing them slightly as he talks.

Art: Brad.

Brad: Yes.

Art: Do *I* exist?

Brad: (*Looks to the hand on his shoulder*). At this point in time, relative to me…yes.

Art: Because you can see me.

Brad: Yes.

Art: And feel me…on your shoulders.

Brad: (*Uneasy*). Yes.

Art: But, if I were to die to you, out of sight….Die in

this instant, like this for example.

Art walks across the kitchen and goes into the adjacent bathroom on the left hand side of the stage and closes the door. We can see Art in the bathroom as well as Brad at the kitchen table although they cannot see each other. Art places both hands and his face against the bathroom door.

Art: Brad…you can hear me.

Brad: Yes.

Art: You cannot see me, however.

Brad: That's right.

Art: Brad…

An extended silence.

Kelly enters the kitchen silently and sits at the table, pouring herself a cup of coffee. They exchange a glance and Kelly motions to him to continue.

Art: Brad…are you still there?

Brad: Yes.

Art: Good, so you're taking a leap of faith that I am actually behind this door. Your mind is processing a familiar voice, which in turn, your conscious mind is using to construct a rational situation you can understand that tells you even though you do not have visual proof of my existence, I indeed *do*, I indeed *am* in existence.... And you, me. Together, we are in an ether of like-existence, sharing it at the same point in space-time. Processing each other's existence on our similar, shared terms.

Brad runs his hands over his face, looks at Kelly.

Art: And this is my other point: This is the core of human connection in this universe. This simultaneous definition of existence between two people, a common understanding that the other person has defined your existence in the exact same way at the exact time in history as you have defined theirs…it's truly a beautiful thing, a mathematical phenomenon in terms of probability in this universe that intelligent beings would not only come to exist, but share this beautiful thing.

Kelly lowers her brow and looks at Brad. Brad shrugs his shoulders slightly.

Art: But with this, Brad, with this connection comes a responsibility. Everything important, everything significant in our lives comes with responsibility. It's what we must all take on, it's what we must all understand…To understand each other, to respect each other's existences, and furthermore, to allow ourselves to feel love for another person even though our minds tell us, everything tells us, with the exception of our hearts…that everything is temporary….This is an important distinction to understand throughout your work. I want to make this point. I want to make this clear. Do you see the distinction, Brad?

Brad: I think I'm beginning to.

Art exhales and leans more of his weight against the door. He reaches down to his belt buckle, releases it, and steps out of his pants. He's now in his shirt and boxer shorts. He places both hands on the wall above his head and looks to the ground.

Art: Brad, I'm going to stay in here for a few more minutes to make my point. We will continue this pseudo-existence between us. I think this will help you in revising? You deserve the best grade possible.

Brad: Yes, I think so.

Brad gets up from the table, pours himself another cup of coffee, and begins pacing the kitchen.

Art: Good. I hope I wasn't too abstract.

Brad: Ahh…no?

Art: Is that a question?

Brad: I'm not sure.

Kelly shakes her head.

Art: So you generally feel things are going well in the class?

Brad: It's one of my favorite classes actually, I mean, I really enjoy your lectures.

Art turns on the faucet and splashes water on his face.

Art: And...

Brad: Well, I don't know -- you know, it's better than calculus.

Art: I suppose it's hard to study with social activities and girls and everything. Your girlfriend?

Brad: Ah, don't have one right now, really.

Art takes off his shirt. He lies down on the bathroom floor and begins strained attempts at sit-ups.

Brad: But, yeah, drinking gets in the way sometimes....The social stuff. But it's cool.

Art: (*Increasingly out of breath*) The social stuff can be a distraction, I know...believe me, I know....When I was your age, I mean. I really liked the social stuff and drugs sometimes too...do you smoke grass? I'm sure you kids do. You don't have to answer that--

He slaps his stomach twice, exhales.

Art: --what's important is that you have *pleasure* in your life even if you have to find ways to create it out of nothing, sometimes *that*, unfortunately, requires some breaking of rules....It's better than dying unfulfilled in a house that looks exactly like your neighbor's (*Nervous laugh*).

Art grunts loudly as he attempts another sit-up. Kelly gets up and walks slowly, silently towards the bathroom door.

Brad: Um, I think I agree.

Satisfied, Art pops back up, catches his breath and leans against the door, hands supporting him above his head.

Art: (*Still breathing heavily*) Unfortunately you *have* to break the rules...the alternative is just too depressing. I'm sorry, this is a bit off the subject. Do you like to swim after classes?

Kelly has now reached the bathroom door. She's standing inches from it, staring at the door and at her unseen father.

Art curls up his boxers and wedges them tightly up into his butt, creating an almost tribal-like man thong. He begins doing standing push-ups against the door.

Brad: Are you ok in there? Seems like you're a little out of breath.

Art: (*Rapidly*) Fine. Fine, really…do me a favor, read the first paragraph, page seven, quick…now.

Confused, Brad grabs his paper and reads.

Brad: Ahh, about Mill, Russell, God…what?

Art: Yes! Quickly. Now.

Kelly's hands are on her hips, she has positioned her ear to the door.

Brad: Ahh, that he "rejected the First Cause argument for the existence of God after reading a passage in Mill's *Autobiography* in which that child reported--

Art: Yeah! Keep going. That's it!

Brad: "--reported: My father taught me that the question 'Who made me?' cannot be answered, since it immediately suggests the further question, 'Who made God?'"

Art: Yes…*who made God*…now we're getting somewhere…

Art lets out an involuntary moan as he stops the push-ups and attempts to catch his breath once again. Kelly backs away from the door slightly.

Brad: What is *wrong*, Professor?

Art: Ah, nothing, that's perfect, perfect, that was

really good. Just moved my back wrong, sciatic nerve, sorry.

Art pulls his pants back up and throws more water on his face and neck. He looks in the mirror, fixes his hair, takes a deep breath and opens the door...

Art: Holy Christ! (*He jumps back and trips on the toilet*).

Kelly: Am I interrupting something?

He catches himself.

Art: Hi sweetie. Ah, no, not at all. I didn't know you were here -- just a session with Brad here with his paper on realism.

She studies him, then turns and walks back towards the table. She sits as Art follows her into the kitchen.

She takes her index finger and starts aimlessly picking at her cuticles.

Kelly: You seemed to really like that passage about... who was it, Mill?

Art: It's an important concept.

Kelly: What is?

Art: The concept about where we come from...who made us...questioning it, at least.

Kelly: You mean, like for example, who made me?

Art: Well, maybe not literally, but yes.

Kelly: Who made me…as in, did *you* make me? That question cannot be answered according to Brad's little paper here because that immediately suggests the further question who made you, etcetera, etcetera, etcetera *(She gets up and walks to him, getting closer)* until the ultimate question arises: *who made God?*

Art looks at her silently. So does Brad.

Kelly: Which means, in turn, who really *is* my creator? (*She looks him in the eye*). Implying that my creator is more than just you. I come from something above you, beyond you, greater than you, more perfect than you…is that what Mill might say? In essence, something a little…less…flawed?

She stares at him. Brad stares at him as well, then to her. No one speaks. She turns slowly to the kitchen table and sits.

She takes a napkin and starts wrapping it tightly around her index finger. She pulls on it hard then unravels it.

Art: *Kelly…*

She starts again, this time winding it around both her index finger and her middle finger. Harder and faster.

They watch her like timid children.

And suddenly she…

…stops.

Brad: You ok?

She unravels, and folds the napkin into a perfect triangle, placing it on the corner of the table.

She pushes the chair back and stands.

Kelly: I'll leave you two.

And with this she starts up the stairs as the stage lights fade.

Bad Blood Better

Saturday, 10:03 AM

The stage lights come up. A bedroom. Posters of rock bands on the wall. Frank is wearing only his boxers. He walks to the mirror and looks at himself. He motions to remove his boxer shorts but stops and instead moves to the bed and lies down, staring at the ceiling for a moment before his right hand moves into his shorts.

Suddenly the door opens. He jumps up.

Frank: What the hell are you doing!

Kelly walks directly for the dresser in the corner. She barely glances at him.

Kelly: If you're going to do that, at least lock the door. (*Then*) Where's my underwear?

Frank: Get outta here! Why would I have your underwear?

He scrambles for his pants, putting them on, then a T-shirt.

Kelly: One of your friends stole my favorite pair from my drawer -- I know he did, and don't try to deny it.

Frank: Just get out of here, please.

Kelly: And I don't even want to know what the hell he'd do with them, or god forbid, you, but I *know* you guys smell them in the crotch--

Frank: *Me?*

Kelly: --and when they get crusty. (*Then*) You think you know your siblings and then something like puberty happens, and he's taken your underwear.

She picks up a bottle of lotion on the bedside table.

Kelly: Or just this.

Frank: Do I have to ask you again?

Kelly: Give me my underwear.

Frank: I don't *have* your underwear.

Kelly stops, regards him, then decides to sit on the bed.

Kelly: Are you sure?

Frank: Yes.

A long beat until…

Kelly: I think you should close the door.

Frank: Why?

Kelly: Because dad will hear us yelling then he'll come up here and ask us what all the fuss is about and I don't want to deal with that.

She lies down on his bed.

Kelly: I have something to tell you. It's pretty important.

Frank: I doubt it.

Kelly: It's why I wanted you to close the door.

Frank: *What.*

Kelly: I think…maybe you should just come lie down on the bed with me…like brother and sis.

Frank: No.

Kelly: Yes.

She stretches her hands above her head and extends her bare feet, pointing her toes towards the opposite wall, an exhale.

Kelly: Yes. It's pretty important. Like I said.

Frank: I think what ever you have to tell me, just tell me and get out.

She regards this for a moment, before...

Kelly: I'm your sister, right?

He cocks his head, waiting.

Kelly: Have you ever wondered where you come from?

Frank: What do you *want*?

Kelly: It's just that we assume a lot. You know what I mean?

Frank: Assume what?

Kelly: In life. It seems like we just take it for granted that our parents tell us who we are, where we came from, showing us pictures of when we were little and all that...

He looks to her then starts picking up clothes.

Kelly: Sometimes I think: do we just accept these things or do we have a responsibility to ourselves to dig a little deeper...maybe for no other reason than for the sake of digging is what I'm trying to get at, I guess.

Frank: I thought you were looking for your underwear.

Kelly: I mean how do we really know? I mean, really….Doesn't that bother you?

Frank: No, not really.

Kelly: I just think we're set up to move along life in certain ways. You know…a blind faith which isn't always that bad, kind of like "ignorance is bliss," along those lines to --

Frank: If you're trying to tell me something, then just please…

Kelly: -- you know, to make it safer for us…for our minds to handle things that would otherwise be unpleasant.

Kelly looks to him then pushes the rim of her all ready low riding jeans down another inch. She inspects her stomach, her hipbone.

Frank: You know something, so tell me.

Kelly: Unfortunately.

Frank: It's bad.

Kelly: I'm afraid so.

Frank walks slowly and sits on the edge of the bed.

Frank: I gather your underwear's not missing.

Kelly: Always a joke when pain's around the corner.

Frank: Who said pain was around the corner?

Kelly: It's always around the corner it's just a matter of how far off.

Frank: (*Quickly*) It's mom and dad.

Kelly: I'm afraid it has more to do with you, than them so much.

He stands.

Frank: Ok, not interested.

Kelly: We're not your real family.

He stops.

Kelly: You were adopted. When you were about two, but mom and dad didn't really know how old you actually were. Your real mom and dad are unknown, and I just found out because I overheard them talking when they thought you and I were out of the house.

She stops, waiting for a response. Nothing.

Kelly: But I know the thing that sucks is that everything you've come to learn about your life, where you've come from, your identity, when you look in the mirror and think you see a bit of dad in your brow, a little of mom in your lips, that they conceived you and you were born into this family … all of that doesn't exist…at least not in the way you've come to understand it in your life.

She shakes her head as if disgusted with the whole scenario.

Kelly: I'm sorry…I really am. You're someone else's blood. But as far as I've been taught in life, blood is not the same as love. You can have one without the other, I think.

He finally moves, if only slightly, as if sizing up an enemy.

Frank: Does this mean I wasn't born Catholic?

Kelly: Trying to call my bluff or something?

Frank: God, you're pathetic. Am I the only one in this household who notices the spiraling behavior?

Kelly: Spiraling?

Frank: Yeah, *downward*…and quite honestly, you can be the worst. Out of neglect or boredom, who knows, but with the three boys a week in and out of your room…(*He stops*)…I mean what is it, Kelly? What is it in your life that's making you so unhappy because believe it or not, I'm actually interested.

She looks at him for a long moment and says nothing until she begins crying, heavily.

He sits on the bed next to her.

Frank: What is it?

She continues to cry, wiping her hand across her eyes. He places his hand on her forehead.

Frank: What happened to you?

Kelly: I just feel so sad for you. That your own parents would betray you like that.

Frank: (*Rolls his eyes*) Oh, come on, Kelly.

Kelly: I mean, parents, maternal or not -- as adults they should offer the truth to their children. There's nowhere else to turn in the world, if you don't have your parents. (*She places her hand on his leg and looks up at him*). I've never felt so sorry for you. I know that's a horrible thing to say, but it's true.

He removes her hand from his leg and walks over to the closet where he pulls out a bottle of J&B and a shot glass. He places these on his desk and begins to pour himself a shot.

Kelly sits up slowly, watching.

Frank: You're almost convincing.

Kelly: What, stashing dad's bottles now?

Frank: I need a drink.

Kelly: Dad thinks you've been drinking too much but hasn't told mom...(*Then*)...The truth is always convincing...I'm sorry Frank, I really am. I wish I weren't the one who had to tell you.

Frank: Finding out I'm adopted wouldn't be much of a blow. I mean, if you really take the time to dissect it. (*Takes a shot*) I don't know what's more pathetic, you barging into my room or the fact that I'm drinking because of it.

Kelly: Maybe your drinking has more to do with the fact that what I'm saying actually makes some sense...but I guess it's easier to blame what's in front of you.

Frank: (*He drops both elbows on the table and leans toward her*) Maybe we should just talk about why you really came in here.

Kelly: The reason is because I thought you should know, and I thought it should come from me because it wasn't going to come from them...(*Then*) But I'm sure it's not about love. I'm sure they still love you --

Frank takes another shot. He exhales and walks toward the bed and stands over her.

Kelly: - - I mean, always have. Of course. Because like I said, it's not always about blood.

Frank: Making people feel uncomfortable is like a sport to you.

Kelly: I'm afraid this time I'm telling the truth.

Frank: (*To himself*) This is not my family...

Kelly: See? Kind of makes sense, doesn't it...I think maybe you should have another shot, it'll make you feel better - get through this part.

He stares at her. She stares back...she's not smiling, she's wiping her eyes. He turns quickly for the door.

Frank: I'm going downstairs to talk to them.

He's about to grab the doorknob when she gets up quickly and cuts him off.

Kelly: Wait. I don't think that's such a good idea at this point.

Frank: Give me one good reason as to why not. (*He laughs again*)...Talk about calling your bluff.

She retracts and starts crying again, walks to the dresser.

Kelly: There's something I haven't told you yet. Just hear me out and then you can go, do what you have to do.

She pours herself a shot and drinks it, then pours one more and drinks that too. She looks to the ground.

Kelly: I'm not your sister.

Frank: Right, got it.

He reaches for the bottle.

Kelly: I mean I'm your sister…just not blood.

Frank: Yeah, you made that clear.

Kelly: No, what I'm saying is that I am too. It's not just you, I've known for about a year…I'm sorry. I just, I found out that they were going to tell you and I wanted you to hear it from me instead of from them because they were going to pull you into a therapist's office to tell you like they did me and it's just the most horrible situation and I didn't want that for you. I just felt it was my responsibility to you as your sister. I would just kill myself if I knew you couldn't count on me for that.

He takes another shot.

Frank: Life just isn't the same without some type of drama is it, Kelly? But you know what? It spills over onto your family, too, and it's exhausting. And your friends. Not to mention the hordes of letter jackets that come through these halls every night carrying their own shoes trying not to make a sound, which is pointless with the eventual moaning.

Kelly: It's not fair to bring letter jackets into this.

Frank: You're going to lecture me on fairness?

Kelly: It's not about lecturing, it's just about the truth…(*Then*)…I guess I'm just glad things are on the table and we have each other to lean on. That makes me feel better.

He looks at her for a moment.

Frank: You actually think I believe you.

Kelly: I was in denial for a month, Frank. I didn't believe them either.

Frank: Then I should just talk to them, right?

Kelly: No. Not now. Let it play its course…things will all work out.

Frank: That's your advice.

Kelly: Really, it's best to take these things in phases, let it sink in a little bit now, then come back to it later. In phases is what I did with it.

She begins to walk to the futon.

Frank: I think you have problems is what I think --

Kelly: They still love us.

Frank: --but you don't even know it…or care if you do. In fact I think you like it, keeps you interested in this house that *bores* you so. *So* dramatic, poor suburban girl with her college paid for and her two hundred dollar shoes.

Frank leans against the dresser, grabs the bottle.

Frank: You're hopeless…is the room spinning?

Kelly: This *house* is spinning…where've you been?

She sits on the futon. A folded blanket sits in the middle of it.

Frank: I think maybe I shouldn't have had the shots.

Kelly: No, you should have. Shots help to numb the pain. And there might be lots of it, so it's ok, you know.

Frank watches her settle onto the futon — adjusting the blanket slightly. She looks to the door, then to Frank.

Kelly: I really didn't mean to interrupt you. You know.

Frank: What.

Kelly: Earlier.

Frank: As if it matters.

Kelly: Sometimes that can help relieve stress. You probably need the stress reliever, is what you're thinking at this point, I mean with the bomb that's just been dropped.

Frank: The art of it, Kelly, is knowing when to lay off.

Kelly: I do love you, you know. I always will. We're the ones in the same boat.

He looks around the room, exhales.

Kelly: Maybe we should get a little rest.

She leans against the arm of the futon and lies down.

Kelly: Come here and sit with me…like brother and sis.

Frank: Why?

Kelly: So we can talk…you don't want to sit by the dresser all day.

A moment until…he walks to the futon and sits at the other end.

Kelly: Afraid of your own sister?

Frank: You would be too.

Kelly: I think a little nap will do us some good, I mean, after all we've been through this morning. Not knowing who you really are can be exhausting, trust me.

She matter of factly unbuttons her jeans and begins to take them off.

He quickly looks to the ceiling.

The jeans drop to a crumpled pile on the floor. She then takes off her t-shirt and drops this to the floor as well. She is now in her panties and bra.

Frank: *(Still looking at the ceiling)* What are you doing?

Kelly: Life is going to be hard for us, Frank…(*Then*) I don't like clothes, you know that. I'm taking a nap.

She takes the blanket and puts it over herself.

Kelly: We're going to need to do what we can to survive…. Maybe even break some rules. To get by, I mean, just for the sake of happiness.

He shifts away from her.

Kelly: Life can just be a fucking drag is what I think. Do you have a smoke? --

Frank: *No.*

Kelly: -- and on top of that, boring. I'm not sure what's worse. Looks like we have a combination. So you get to a point in your life and realize something has to be done to get through it…or at least make it interesting--

She fumbles under the blanket momentarily before pulling her hand out, revealing her underwear.

Kelly: --because whoever said life was short had to be a clown…

She drops these on top of the jeans and t-shirt. Then back under for a moment before she pulls out her bra, this too drops to the floor. She is completely covered by the blanket.

Kelly: At some point, you just look at life and say, "fuck it," -- I'm the one who has to survive in all this. And what I find is about after the third or fourth beer is when it really sinks in and it makes sense to me: "I didn't create it, I just have to survive it." And Frank, when you really understand *that* you can get through it and do things without guilt, you know?

She slides down further and lays her head back; her hands disappear under the blanket.

Frank: Maybe you should keep your hands out, you know, where I can see them...

Kelly: Do you know what my IQ is?

Frank: 132.

Kelly: That's right. 132. Last time I checked that was pretty damned up there so I have things to say.

Frank: I'm sure you do, but how about going to your room and do this?

Kelly: It's just about breaking the rules sometimes... *come on,* Frank, you're such a bookworm.

Frank: I *like* being a bookworm. Is that so *boring*?

Kelly: I don't think you're boring. I just think you need some spark in your life...(*Then*) Look over here.

Frank: I don't think so, thank you.

Kelly: You really are afraid of your own sister. I think that's so funny.

Frank: Yeah I know, hilarious.

Kelly looks at him, Frank stares at the ground. Suddenly we see some movement under the blanket between Kelly's legs. This catches Frank's attention where he finally looks over.

Frank: *Jesus.*

Kelly: What, you think you're the only one in this house that gets off…I mean, come on.

Frank: Always have to make things uncomfortable.

Kelly: Oh, come on…you can't see anything, you dope.

More movement under the blanket.

Kelly: I mean, you don't really even know if I'm *doing* anything. I could just be scratching my thigh…I have a rash on my thigh that *needs* scratching.

Frank: Can't you just decide to leave me alone?

Kelly: Where's the fun in that?

She closes her eyes. He stares at the ground waiting for her to speak; she doesn't. He moves his eyes slightly to see what she's doing.

She opens one eye, seeing him. He looks away quickly. She grins and moves her left leg out from under the blanket and places it on the floor — letting out a subtle moan.

He jumps up and walks to the other side of the room. She laughs.

Kelly: I'm kidding! Get over here, I'm messing with you. God! Sit down.

Frank: Just, put some clothes on…something.

Kelly: Fine. If you can't handle it, just come sit down.

Frank: Put something on first.

Kelly: You can't sit down first?

Frank: You do this with all of us -- just stop pushing us all the time.

She regards this then reaches for her underwear. She maneuvers under the blanket, putting them back on.

Kelly: There. Happy?

He walks back to the futon and sits, facing her.

Frank: Thank you. (*Then*) Why do you always want to make people feel uncomfortable?

Her hand emerges from under the blanket, holding her underwear. She drops them onto the pile again. He doesn't see this.

Kelly: I don't. I just, sometimes I like to forget about things.

Frank: Funny way to go about it.

Kelly: Worked, didn't it? You didn't think about being adopted for what, a whole couple minutes. It's a good way to get by in life.

Frank: Again with that?

Kelly: I just don't understand why you would be so traumatized if I actually *did* play with myself. Like mom and dad throwing a complete tizzy over seeing my nipples…just because society's uptight like that, why should *I* have to be that way? Answer me that, Frankie, and I'll put on all my clothes and leave you be.

Frank: You don't have to pull a shock protest every time to make a point. We'll still listen to you if you don't.

Kelly: No, Frank! That's where you're wrong. I *don't* get listened to. I just don't. Mom and dad don't listen to me, they never did -- they just tell me things I should or shouldn't do, and it's not fair.

She retracts, then…

Kelly: This family *really* has its problems…I mean really, and I'm not just saying that because no one listens to me.

Frank: That's in your head.

Kelly: No, I really mean it.

Frank: Well, so do a lot of families -- deal with it.

Kelly: But it's not just that, I mean I think dad…I think, I kinda worry about him.

Frank: Why?

She hesitates…

Kelly: Forget it.

Frank: No, what.

She sits up, holding the blanket over herself.

Kelly: I walked down to the kitchen when he was having a session with one of his students and he was in the bathroom.

Frank: Yeah, so.

Kelly: No, I mean he was like *conducting* his session from the bathroom. His student was at the table and they were talking while he was in the bathroom.

Frank: So what.

She looks to him for a moment.

Kelly: Well, I'm not sure how to put this…but he was like making weird noises as he was talking, like really breathing heavily. I was freaked out.

Frank: What kind of noises?

Kelly: Like heavy panting, breathing really heavily.

Frank: Panting?

Kelly: And he was yelling at his student, making him read from this passage about the creation of God or something like a crazy priest….It was really kind of freaky, like I didn't know who he was.

Frank: Doesn't sound *that* odd, I mean, aside from being in the bathroom.

Kelly: It was though. It actually kind of scared me. He didn't seem like dad, it was like he was…predatory.

Frank: *Predatory?*

Kelly: And for a moment I just really felt scared for us, for this family.

A long beat as she reaches for her pile of clothes and starts to put them on under the blanket.

Frank: Well…I'm sorry.

Kelly: Yeah, me too…and then I just started kind of yelling at him, really confronting him saying things to hurt him like questioning him as my creator, all this crazy stuff I didn't even know what I was talking about…and that made me even more scared but I just kept doing it.

She pulls the blanket off her, fully clothed.

Kelly: Makes me think that sometimes this family is just going to split up…I always think that when I wake up in the morning.

She folds the blanket into a perfect square and places it on the end of the futon.

Kelly: Weird, huh…

Frank: No.

She looks at the blanket from a different angle then adjusts it, tightening the corner, flattening out a small wrinkle. She looks at it for a moment, then up at Frank.

Kelly: I never mean to harass you. I mean, I *do*, but not in a bad way.

He's looking at the blanket.

Kelly: And I wasn't really playing with myself -- and we're not adopted. That was all bullshit.

She gets up and adjusts her jeans, top.

Kelly: You handled yourself pretty well though, considering all I threw at you.

Frank: You make it sound like we're not going to make it through the next week…as a family, I mean.

Kelly: It's not that…It's just a feeling of false security. This house and this neighborhood always seemed like they were holding something that was about to happen. Like if something bad happened here, it would be *really* bad. Because of all the order… or something. Like we deserve it. (*Then*) It actually creeps me out, if you wanna know the truth.

She walks towards the bedside table….

Kelly: I don't know, I guess what I'm saying is --

…grabs the bottle of lotion…

Kelly: -- that I've just expected it to fall apart for as long as I can remember.

…and tosses it on his lap.

Kelly: Back to business, Frankie.

She turns to leave as the lights fade.

We Will Begin Our Descent

Saturday, 11:30 AM

A home office. There are floor to ceiling cedar bookshelves. A large desk is positioned diagonally in the corner with the chair facing us. Books and papers are spread about the desk in such a manner as to suggest an intellect not concerned with order for the sake of order.

There is a worn, brown leather sofa along one wall upon which Art sits. A stack of papers and a red pen lay on the sofa next to him as he sits forward, looking at the ground between his feet.

Patterson is standing with his back to us, hands crossed, staring at the rows of books lining the wall.

Patterson: --as Chair of the department I *have* to confront this.

Art: It's a complaint, fine, but it's alleged.

Patterson turns from the books and looks to him,

starting to pace about the room.

Patterson: But also because we've known each other for ten years.

Art: Then I'd hope you'd understand this is a circumstance of misinterpretation.

Patterson: Of what Art. Of language? Of *what*? I'm trying to understand what you're saying, because I want to give you the benefit of a doubt.

Art: Body language, intentions--

Patterson: This student--

Art: -- and me, everything.

Patterson: - - she outlined in her complaint that you touched her on the shoulders more than once, what does that mean?

Art: It means that I touched her more than once.

Patterson: Ok.

Art: On the *shoulders*.

Patterson: Playing that card's as good as digging your own hole.

Art: I didn't do anything wrong.

Patterson: That's still up for debate.

Art: Look, I have a session with a student and by nature I become invested in that student, in the material, in where the learning process takes us. Being impassioned is vital to the educator and the one being educated. It's why I'm a professor, it's not the research or being published…it's just not.

Patterson: I do believe that.

A pause…

Art: I think it's the youth of the students is what it is --

Patterson: What about touching her on the shoulder, what about that? Why do you have to *do* that, I mean, I know you're a good person.

Art: -- To remember being that age, what it felt like physically, your body, and having absolutely no idea what it means to be an adult. To be around students that age is, it's really something, it really is.

Patterson: If you ever get questioned about this, don't start talking this way.

Art: It's a free pass out of being forty-five, out of this house is what it is…I love this house, don't misinterpret that, but we're taught to say what we don't mean and not say what we mean and certainly not *do* what we feel because of the consequences.

Patterson stops pacing, looks up at the books on the shelves and cocks his head.

Patterson: Art…you don't have to *say* everything in life --

Art: There's just too much at stake in our lives — the threat of rejection - to live it the way we want to live it and that kills me, it really does.

Patterson: --and certainly not *act* on everything.

Art: You know what I mean?…(*Then*) With a lawyer around every corner it's just easier to find a good way to suppress what we might rather want to explore. Let's live in fear of losing things, right?…Face it, it's why you're here right now staring at my goddamned books.

Patterson: What does that mean?

Art: It's more comfortable not to have to look at me right now, and don't deny it, because I've known you for ten years.

Art looks at his papers, picks up his pen, then places it back down. Patterson turns around to face him; they regard each other for a moment.

Art: I just placed my hand on her shoulder a few times as we talked….that's it. Like I said, misinterpreted… I'm harmless, I'm just a professor with a family.

Patterson: Why do you think that would be misinterpreted?

Art: Because it can be. Because she's a nineteen-year-old girl, I'm her professor, and we had a private study session, as I do with most of my students.

Patterson: She felt uncomfortable, though. Why would that be, if it were an innocent touch to the shoulder?

Art: Maybe she was molested by her father.

Patterson: Be serious.

Art: I am.

Patterson: No, you're not.

Art: She was with a middle-aged professor, alone in a subordinate role.

Patterson: That's your answer?

Art: Yes --

Patterson: *Jesus…*

Art: A society might dictate that the situation by its very nature *has* to be harboring intent, from at least one side…if not both.

Patterson: Both?

Art: It's impossible for me to regulate myself based on how society might want me to behave in such a situation…Which is, by the way, not the same as saying I did anything wrong. I didn't.

Patterson: You can't blame this on society. That's a child's argument.

Art: I did nothing wrong, so what's to blame?

Patterson: Or *who*.

Art: Don't interrogate me. Besides, you know I didn't do anything wrong.

Patterson: I'm not interrogating you, but we're not getting anywhere -- you have a way of talking in circles.

Art: That's because there's nowhere to get.

Patterson: There you go again.

Art: There I go what again?

Patterson exhales, then sits next to him on the couch.

Patterson: I've known you for ten years.

Art: I hate it when people say things like that—

Patterson: There's one thing that's killing you and

you know it.

Art: --it always segues into something like "something's *killing* you and you know it."

Patterson: I think you know what it is.

Art: No I don't.

Patterson: It's this house.

Art looks at the bookshelf for a moment, then breathes deeply. He takes the red pen and starts flicking it quickly between his fingers.

Art: You don't have to *say* everything in life.

Patterson: Always with a joke.

Art: I mean really…

Patterson: Well?

Art: You don't have everything figured out.

Patterson: And this neighborhood too.

Art: This house has nothing to do with this.

Patterson: I want to believe you did nothing wrong, Art. But if you're not being completely honest with me and the student decides to get a lawyer, which she hasn't yet, Sara would leave you. You know that.

Art: What makes you think it would take a tragedy for her to leave?

Patterson: You're full of shit, and you know it. Sara loves you.

Art: You can be in love without being fulfilled — you just don't want to face the alternative. There's still a lot of hours to fill every day -- it's what they don't tell you at the altar.

Patterson: God, you can be depressing.

Art: You think I don't know that?

Patterson: I know you know it.

Art: It depresses me just knowing I *depress* people.

Patterson: Well, at least you realize it.

Art: *That's* what depresses me.

Patterson: I rest my case.

Art: When I wake in the morning before Sara gets up, it kills me to think we're going to be happy for *thirty* more years…and that has nothing to do with love, it just doesn't.

Patterson: Marriage is work. *That's* what they don't tell you at the altar.

Art: It's not just marriage…life should never get too easy. There *is* such a thing as being too safe and too comfortable…especially in a neighborhood like this.

Patterson: You think Sara's not fulfilled.

Art: You've got to do *something* to fill all those hours, even if it means walking on a tightrope…(*He exhales and runs his fingers through his hair*) Feels great when there's a long fall on both sides…but I've passed that on to my daughter, which I don't like. My son got more of Sara in him; good for him.

Patterson: That's destructive behavior.

Art: Only if you don't control it. I'm a shell without them and I know that…(*Then*) No, she's not fulfilled, and it makes me feel like a failure.

Patterson: You think it's because of you.

Art: She has a stunning mind and I know she has regrets in her life about not seeing parts of the world. These lawns remind you of the choices you've made…they're just so unforgiving.

Patterson: Never thought of them that way.

Art: She wanted to live abroad. We didn't. We ended up creating a cushioned life for ourselves.

Patterson: That's what people strive for.

Art: It's a mistake. But we've created a good life for our kids, even though I've created it on a sheet of glass.

Patterson: I know you love your family.

Art: I love them more than anything. But it seems like such a struggle to keep them happy.

Patterson: Don't take this the wrong way, Art, but as long as I've known you it seems your struggle has been to keep *you* happy. You try to be what is expected of you, and I've always gotten the feeling you're treading water….Swimming upstream, really.

Art: Well, which is it?

Patterson: Don't be a smartass —

Art: Well, am I treading or going upstream? Two very different things.

Patterson: --*on top* of being depressing.

Art inhales and rubs his eyes.

Art: I don't want to look like my neighbors.

Patterson: That over simplifies the situation.

Art: It takes a lot of work not to -- I mean, you can only do so much with stucco.

Patterson: You use this neighborhood as your scapegoat. This neighborhood's not you.

Art: My family sees right thought me…especially my daughter. She *is* me. I know it. She knows I think this house is built on a bed of glass, and I swear sometimes she's out to shatter it.

Patterson: Why would that be?

Art: You're not listening to me.

Patterson: What?

Art: She *is* me. It's what we do.

Patterson: The only ones who can shatter it are you and Sara. And more specifically, *you,* Art. *Your* actions, because know it or not, you're the center of this family and if it's going to get destroyed, it's going to be you who does it.

Art folds his arms to his chest.

Art: What are we going to do about the accusation?

Patterson: I'm going to have a follow-up conversation with her, tell her we talked, and explain to her what we discussed — how actions can be misinterpreted. I think we'll be ok.

Art: Thank you.

Patterson: I'm *not* doing you a favor. I just happen to believe you -- I've known you long enough.

Art: Think she'll get a lawyer?

Patterson: If she hasn't by now, I don't think she will. This'll only go as far as the three of us.

Art rubs his face, looks to the ceiling.

Patterson: But I could be wrong.

Art: (*Looks at him quickly*) Thanks for the confidence.

Patterson: Well, I could be.

Art: My family can't know about this, they just can't. Even though I haven't done anything wrong.

Patterson gathers his coat and walks to the door.

Patterson: Good. Think about that, because if you're going to believe that the only way to define your life as interesting is to walk on a tight rope because these lawns are too much for you to handle, then eventually, someday you're going to do something and you *will* pull this family down with you--

He puts on his coat and opens the door.

Patterson: --and then you're finished.

Art leans forward.

Art: I'm a good person, Patterson.

Patterson: Don't say it, Art -- *show* it.

And with that he leaves and closes the door. The lights fade.

Knowing Sri Lanka

Saturday, 2:15 PM

The master bedroom. There is a bed in the middle with a flower pattern bedspread and a mass produced print of Picasso's "Old Guitar-Player" above it.

On the floor is a dark blue, yet somewhat faded carpet that would suggest a year or more of neglect. There is a bathroom on the left side of the stage which is connected to this bedroom although we cannot see into it.

Sara wears sweatpants and a tank top. She sits in the chair in the corner and speaks to an unseen voice in the bathroom.

Sara: This is about different things, I don't think you've ever quite gotten that…I don't hold it against you though.

Voice (*O.S.*): I want to be sensitive too, I do. You know I don't mean not to be.

Sara: But we're responsible for it, we have a responsibility to create our own happiness. There's nothing *wrong* with that.

Voice (*O.S.*): No one else is going to do it.

Sara: You're repeating what I said. You really need to think for yourself.

Voice (*O.S.*): I'm *agreeing*, not repeating. I do, I can think for myself.

Sara: I spend five hours every week with the charity and I keep the family fed. Frank and Kelly have a good home, a normal, Middle American home -- they can be thankful for that.

Voice (*O.S.*): You gotta look at the big picture, you're right. You know, I think that's all good and I think you have a great outlook on life, the surroundings you know, even if sometimes they're not what we'd always hoped for in our lives. But even aside from all that--

The toilet flushes.

Sara: What?

Voice (*O.S.*): --I still think you're one of the most beautiful women I've ever seen.

Sara gets up and walks to the mirror above the dresser. She places a strand of her hair behind her ear, cocks her head then runs her index fingers under both of her eyes, pinching the skin back momentarily before pushing her right breast upward, studying it.

Sara: When I was in Journalism school I wanted to live in Vienna after I graduated -- it was my plan. Did I ever tell you that?...Probably not.

The bathroom faucet is turned on, we hear the running water.

Voice (*O.S.*): Did you say something?

Sara: No...You've been in there for almost five minutes.

No answer as her voice meshes with the running water.

Sara: *(Still studying herself in the mirror)* I probably would have met people who have lived in Algeria or worked for the United Nations and have done things, I mean real things, like alleviate epidemics -- not just people who *talk* about those things, like around here...Actually *do*...They say if you surround yourself with successful people you're more inclined to be one yourself. Or at least lead a more interesting life. Some run-off maybe.

The water stops running causing her to come back to the moment. She walks to the bed and sits, then gets up and walks back to the chair and sits again. Her expression shifts...she looks toward the bathroom.

Sara: Quite honestly, this is a little agitating.

Voice (*O.S.*): Did you even hear me? That you're beautiful and interesting...*worldly*, I even think. That's so sexy.

She leans back into the chair.

Sara: That's nice of you, but...

And with that the bathroom door opens, and Brad enters.

Brad: What time is it?

Sara: He won't be home for a while, if that's what you're asking. He had to go to campus.

Brad walks to the door and turns the doorknob.

Sara: It's *locked,* for the third time.

She gets up and walks to him. She places a hand on his chest, releases.

Sara: This isn't going to work if you don't relax. You're making me nervous now. Let's just, maybe we...

Brad: Maybe we should do this faster, you know, just to be safe....Where's Frank and Kelly?

Sara: God, what were we thinking, doing this *here.*

She releases and walks to the bed. He follows her.

Brad: It was *your* idea to come here, we could have gone anywhere…specifically this bed which, no offense, was a bit surprising, but I guess the idea of doing it in the place where the same sex has happened for twenty years could be really good for the orgasm, a lot of them--

Sara: This was stupid.

Brad: --since you know, the brain after all is the key sex organ, although in my case a lot of girls at school have gone out of their way to compliment my *other* organ as really nice, one even called it "beautiful" although she was drunk…they both were.

She puts her hand up.

Sara: *You* need to work on the nervous talking.

He exhales.

Brad: OK, but have you ever heard a girl refer to a guy's junk as beautiful?

Sara: *No.*

Brad: I really took it as a compliment, it made me happy and the whole next day I just felt really good with a lot of confidence. And I have to admit I looked at it in a new way after that.

Sara: How nice.

Brad: I really do think it *is* beautiful and not just because she said it. I guess my point would be that it's great to look at yourself in the mirror and like what you see whether that's started by a fleeting compliment or someone else's desire for you, is not really the point, the point is how you take it and turn it into feeling good about yourself, your current life.

He smiles, proud of his deduction as he reaches down the front of his jeans, adjusting.

Sara: Go sit in the chair.

He does. She lies down on the bed.

Brad: I just want you to be satisfied with this. It's not just about wanting to have sex with you. I want to provide something more for you, like, fulfill a need you have because I sense there's a lot of that, you know, just as people write me off as being just a college kid … I can sometimes surprise people and hit things on the head. Human nature, I guess. So, I guess maybe we should do this?

She sits up.

Sara: You make me sound like a charity.

Brad: Oh, I don't mean to. You know that.

Sara: Like there's such a void I've created for myself

that here I am with you, and thank god, because the life I created for myself is so average…I do *know* people from Sri Lanka, ok?…Because if you think I only matter in this town then, well, you're just too young to know any better--

She pounds a pillow with her fist, fluffing it.

Sara*: --you* still think you can have anything you want in life. What a farce.

Brad: You know I don't think you're charity, I think you're beautiful. Since when has that not cut it?

She sits up on the edge of the bed.

Sara: I have a good life.

Brad: I'm not implying you don't. I--

Sara: Sometimes all you *do* is talk.

He looks at her for a moment.

Brad: Do you love your husband?

She cocks her head at him, raises her eyebrows.

Brad: It's a legitimate question.

She walks to the dresser and begins to re-fold the clothes.

Sara: (*Points to him*) Here's what you don't know…

He rolls his eyes, looks down to the bulge now faltering between his legs.

Sara: We get to a point in our lives where we realize we're one of the relatively unimportant people and when we die, no one will write about us, we don't have a body of hit movies that people can go back to watch, I've written no great novels that will outlive me…it's at that point when you realize that you're faced with the prospect of creating your own purpose that's meaningful to not only yourself, but to at least *someone*.

Brad: Am *I* someone?

She looks at him, then at the shirt she's holding. She finishes folding it and places it in the drawer.

Sara: It's at the point when *that* idea really sinks in, is when you know you have to create some type of experience for yourself…to keep you alive, even if it means breaking some rules--

She closes the drawer and sits back down on the bed. Brad removes his shirt. She watches him as he kneels slowly on the floor before her.

Sara: --because I can't bear to look at all these houses every day --

He places a hand on each of her knees.

Sara: --and still believe I'm an interesting person.

She inhales then looks to the door before looking back down to him. He slides her sweatpants down to her ankles, his head between her thighs.

Sara: Brad.

He looks up.

Brad: Yeah.

Sara: Don't look at me when you do this. No offense.

Brad: Sure, whatever.

Sara: Do you like my panties?

He looks at his chest.

Brad: I *do* and I worked my pecs for thirty minutes yesterday, complete burnout.

Sara: They're new.

She leans back and rests on her elbows.

Sara: Maybe we should turn down the lights.

He moves his head in towards her crotch and appears

to move her panties to the side although we cannot see this directly. His head is there for a moment before Sara's mouth opens slightly and she exhales.

Sara: Oh…

Brad leans in, his head moves about slightly faster. His motion continues, a deliberate repetition.

Sara: Ohhhh shit.

He says something but we cannot make it out, it's a highly muffled response. He doesn't look at her.

Sara: Brad….

His face is all but lost between her thighs. Her body takes over, offering herself to him. Finally she inhales, bites her lower lip and…closes her eyes.

Sara: Oh my god…

Her breathing becomes more rapid. She lets out a slight moan and drops to the bed, her legs raise up, she holds her breath, her legs tense, suspended in the air for a moment until…

A big exhale. She grabs his head, pushing him away. He looks at her as she gets up.

Brad: That was *fast*.

Sara: Yeah.

She pulls her sweatpants back up and walks to the door, checking the doorknob.

Brad: It's locked.

Sara: Just checking.

He walks to her and tries to kiss her but she pulls away.

Brad: I want to have sex.

Sara: I'm not sure that's such a good idea…I think we've been up here for longer than we thought.

Brad: I want to make love to you.

Sara: I don't think so — not now.

She looks at her watch, becoming increasingly nervous again; she walks into the bathroom. The water begins running.

Sara (*O.S.*): You have to leave. I'm sorry.

Agitated, he puts his shirt back on.

Brad: This is bullshit.

He moves about the room looking for his belongings then yells to the bathroom.

Brad: I have *such* an erection right now! You know

how that feels!?

He stops, jams his hand down the front of his jeans and adjusts.

Brad: 'Course you don't.

Sara (*O.S.*): What?

Brad: All you care about is *not* being bored--

Sara: (*O.S.*) I can't hear you!

Brad: --In your little gingerbread house. God, what a nightmare.

He looks at the bathroom door, then at the other door.

Brad: What are you *doing* in there?

Sara (*O.S.*): I'm cleaning up, I'll be out in a second -- don't leave *yet!*

Brad: This *is* bullshit. I'm not forty, I can't just roll over and read *The Times*.

He walks to her dresser, opens the drawer, and pulls out a pair of her panties. He moves the chair from the corner of the room to the bathroom door, jamming it in place.

Sara (*O.S.*) What was that?

He walks to the opposite side of the bed, away from the audience, and sits. He unbuttons his pants and pulls them down to his knees.

Brad: (*To the bathroom*) Take your time.

He places her panties to his nose and inhales, then reaches down the front of his underwear. He manages three pumps before the door swings open, causing the chair to slide helplessly to the floor.

Sara: Christ!

Brad shoots up, attempting to gather himself.

Sara: Are those my *panties*?

She lunges for them.

They struggle for a moment before she finally wrestles them out of his grasp, causing him to slip and fall against the wall.

Sara: For Christ's sake….I think you should go. Just … get out of here.

He pulls his pants back up.

Brad: Come on, you're mad at me for needing —

Sara: I'm not mad….You should just go.

She places her panties back in the drawer, then sits

on the chair. She walks back to the drawer, takes the panties back out, and throws them in the trash.

He sees this, cocks his head.

She returns to the chair, places her hands in her face and begins crying. He walks to her as he swings his backpack over one shoulder.

Brad: Please, don't. I hate that…I'll go…I'll just go. I have to work on my paper anyway.

She looks up at him as he walks to the door.

Brad: Are you going to be ok? I mean, I thought that felt good.

Sara: It's not *that*.

Brad: What is it?

Sara: You should know something.

Brad: What…?

Sara: It's not just about the houses.

Brad: What?

Sara: You don't *listen* to me.

Brad: Maybe we should talk about this later, like you said.

She gets up and reaches across him, unlocking the door. She looks at him, thinking for a moment, until…

Sara: I think my husband is attracted to you.

She wipes the tears from her eyes. Brad freezes.

Sara: It's just…it's just horrible…I think he would choose to have sex with you if the opportunity arose.

She opens the door and places her hand on his backpack as if to shove him out of the room.

Sara: I just thought you should know, since you spend so much time with him. Your studies, I mean. I just don't want you to get into an awkward situation that may or may not blow up in your face…or mine.

She pushes him lightly out the door.

Sara: I love my family, Brad. And even though it's cookie-cutter, I love this house too. Please remember that.

And with that, she gives him one final nudge and closes the door.

Sara: You know the way out.

The stage lights cut to darkness.

Spy Hole

Saturday, 6:45 PM

Kelly's bedroom. A queen-sized bed is in the middle of the room. Two oversized windows take up one wall and under these sit two plush floor pillow seats. Kelly sits on her bed flipping aimlessly through a magazine as a song plays from her nearby iPod deck.

Her cell phone rings.

She pops her head up and answers it.

Kelly: (*Into phone*) Hi…*No*, let me come down, head around to the back and I'll let you in. *Don't* ring the doorbell.

She clicks the phone and walks out. The music continues.

A few moments later…

She enters with Lisa. Lisa's wearing a black T-shirt and jeans and has a North Face backpack slung over one shoulder. Her hair is a sandy brown and she appears to be about Kelly's age. She's pretty in a tomboyish way.

Kelly: Completely forgot to tell you to come to the back door.

Lisa: It's all right -- I don't think anyone saw me.

Kelly closes the door and locks it. She puts her ear to the door for a moment, then turns toward the windows.

Kelly: Here--

She opens both windows and drags the pillow seats next to them.

Kelly: --sit.

They both sit, each under their own window. Lisa places the backpack on the floor in between her feet and starts to unzip it.

Kelly: So, you go to school here, right? I think that's what Lauren mentioned, the U?

Lisa: Second year. …She's a friend of yours?

Kelly: Yeah.

Lisa: So she knows Greg--

Kelly: Through another person.

Lisa: Greg's cool.

She reaches deep into her backpack, pulls out a clear bag of weed and starts opening it. Kelly gets up and walks across the room. She places her ear against the door.

Lisa: Your parents going to try to come in?

Kelly: No, but my mom's on a particular rage today. I mean, a kid needs a little weed just to manage the stress of living in this *house*.

Lisa takes out components of a two-foot-high water bong and begins assembling it.

Kelly: It's really a medical marijuana issue is what it is. Mental stress.

Lisa: I've been saying that for years.

Kelly: I mean, what's the difference if the pain comes from a tumor or from your family? Is it really that different --

Kelly walks back to her seat and watches her assemble the bong.

Kelly: --a little discriminatory if you ask me. (*Then*) Is that a *hookah*?

Lisa: Yeah.

Kelly: Hmm.

Lisa: I got it from The Gypsy Café, it works really well even though its a bit high maintenance and I had to retrofit it.

Kelly: Yeah, looks like it.

Assembled, Lisa places it on the floor between them. Two long tubes extend from the main shaft, one for each of them. She fills the shaft with water and places a lump of weed at the top tray.

Lisa: Ok, so this stuff is…how should I say it…

Kelly: Stuff's *what*.

Lisa: It's from Oregon and it's like some type of new strain or something.

Kelly: What does that mean?

Lisa: I've had it once before and it's…intense.

Kelly: Intense *how*?

Lisa: Ahh, intense like maybe seeing or hearing things.

Kelly: Hallucinations?

Lisa: Yeah, some people don't handle that real well; they like to have a bit more control. So--

Lisa takes out a lighter and holds it to the lump of weed.

Lisa: --if you let go a bit, you'll enjoy it more.

Kelly: Happy to…

And with that Lisa flicks the lighter and places the flame to the weed. They put their tubes to their mouths and inhale. The water starts to bubble as their chests expand. They hold until they both turn their mouths towards the open windows and exhale.

Lisa closes her eyes for a moment before leaning back into the seat. She takes off her running shoes.

Kelly: God, that's good.

Lisa: Josephine County.

Kelly: Who?

Lisa takes another hit; so does Kelly. They both exhale out the window. Kelly gets up and walks in circles, smelling the air.

Kelly: Can you smell it in here?

She makes a pass by the door, leaning her nose forward, sniffing. She opens the door and sticks her head out.

Kelly: Don't think you can smell it out there.

Lisa: I'd close the door, it's gonna seep out.

She closes the door, stuffs a towel at the base, and sits back down.

They both lean back and extend their legs.

Kelly: Can't wait to get to college so I don't have to worry about this.

Lisa: Little strict?

Kelly: This family has *problems*.

Lisa: Welcome to the club.

Kelly: *This one's* a time bomb -- you have no idea.

Lisa: Nice neighborhood, though.

Kelly: Exactly.

Lisa lights the lump and they take another hit.

Kelly: My dad locks himself in the bathroom and is generally losing it, he really is, and my mom's trying to stop it and they're both freaking out about having to live another thirty years. How fucking depressing is *that*? I mean, talk about having too much time on your hands to think about your own existence. But who can feel sorry for them? Get out of this gingerbread neighborhood already, and go *live*.

Lisa smiles.

Kelly: You know what I mean?

Lisa: Ok, you think you have problems? (*Then*) I barely know you, but whatever.…When I was in middle school, my parents used to have these parties at our house. These big dinner parties where their friends would come over and drink gallons of cocktails before dinner.

She takes another hit. Exhales.

Lisa: So one morning after one of their parties I get up to go to the bathroom. It was a Saturday morning and it was raining. I walked down the hall and the door to their bedroom was open a crack. I looked in and saw another couple sleeping with them. I remember seeing a tangle of legs and arms everywhere and the rain hitting the window. I just stood there.

Kelly: They could've at least shut the door.

Lisa: My parents weren't even next to each other. One on each side of the bed with the other two in the middle.

Kelly: How old were you?

Lisa leans back and looks up at the ceiling for a moment.

She reaches up and grabs at the air, capturing The Thing that's hovering above her head. She holds it for a moment then releases it back into the air.

Lisa: Fourteen.

Kelly's eyes follow the trajectory extending from Lisa's hand, looking for whatever she just released.

Lisa: I realized they were my parents' best friends, Mr. and Mrs. Kent. They kept coming over and I didn't even want to look at them but they always tried to talk to me, asking me questions about school. They were dirty to me and I hated them.

She quickly jerks her head to one side as if avoiding It.

Kelly: I think I saw that. Did something just fly by your face?

Lisa: Yeah.

Kelly: (*Eyes still searching*) So did you ever tell your parents you knew what was up?

Lisa: No. I just remember hating the Kents so much. I remember the last time they left our house -- it was in the afternoon, it was after they had lunch on the patio in the back yard. But there was another storm coming, the kind you can feel in the air when the pressure changes, you can just smell it. Mr. Kent said good-bye to me and I didn't say anything, I just remember saying to myself, I hope they get in a car accident on the way home.

She turns on her side and brings her knees up to her chest.

Kelly: So how long did they keep doing this?

Lisa: That was the last time I ever saw them.

She reaches into the pouch and places a few more buds on the tray. She flicks them a few times with her middle finger.

Lisa: A few days later we were all sitting in the kitchen having breakfast. My mom made this egg casserole that had bacon and cheese in it. It was all foamy but I remember it being good. And we had rubber placemats with oranges on them. They were durable -- they were the only placemats I ever remember having as a kid....The phone rang. My mom answered it and after a few moments she just put the phone on the counter and sat on the ground. My father yelled at her, asking her what was wrong. He got up and took the phone and I remember him just yelling.

Lisa places the flame to the weed and they take another.

Kelly exhales and coughs. She places her hand to her mouth, hunched over, trying to let the burn pass. She finally positions her face to the window and inhales.

Kelly: I think that may be it for me.

Lisa: Forgot to tell you, you probably only need a couple hits. So, Mr. Kent decides to string up a shotgun in his bathtub with a makeshift pulley system. He sits in it wearing a three-piece suit and yanks on the string that's connected to the trigger. Blows his head into a hundred pieces. That's what I heard from some other kid, anyway.

Kelly: *God.*

Lisa: My parents told me he took a bottle of pills. I get why they lied to me, but did they really think I wouldn't find out? Everyone in town knew.

Kelly: Who found him?

Lisa: His wife, three days later. Basically found a body in a suit with no head. Just a bunch of dried up pieces caked to the sides of the bathtub. She'd been on a weekend trip with the girlfriends so it probably stunk to high heaven….Some asshole kid at school said flies had hatched everywhere but he was always full of shit.

Kelly's jaw slowly drops.

Lisa: That house became toxic. I remember walking

to the other side of the street on the way home from school so I wouldn't have to go by it. Just looking at it scared me -- the window to that bathroom faced the street.

Kelly: What did she do, move away?

Lisa: No, had the bathroom cleaned up, redecorated the entire house. But I never saw her again ... she never came over to our house again. I just saw her driving in her car, unpacking groceries in her driveway like a droid. Her face looked different, I remember she started to scare me....The *neighborhood* was toxic after that. But after a couple years I kind of forgot about it, buried it, and moved on with being a kid.

Kelly: Your parents ever talk about it?

Lisa gets up out of her chair. She lifts the window up farther and sits in the sill, breathing in the fresh air. She looks at Kelly, thinking.

Lisa: Lots of information. I barely know you.

Kelly: I don't think you can shock me, not with my family.

Lisa walks over to the iPod deck and starts going through the menu of songs.

Lisa: What do you like?

Kelly: Pretty much everything on there. (*Then*) Why

does that lamp have a heartbeat?

Lisa: (*Without looking up*) It grows a heart when it's exposed to this smoke.

Kelly stares at it.

Lisa: I can stop the heart if I turn it off.

Kelly: *Please.*

She does and selects a new song. The lights in the room dim.

She lies on the bed and positions herself on her side, facing Kelly.

They look at each other in silence as the music plays. The music is otherworldly and they seem to be drifting in it. Riding it. And this goes on for a moment until…

Kelly: What'd your parents do? I mean, that was your dad's best friend.

Lisa grabs another pillow and places it under her head, embracing it.

Lisa: A few weeks after the funeral is when I noticed the hole…in the edge of the door frame in my bedroom. It was the door that led from my bedroom to the bathroom I shared with my parents.

Kelly: Hole?

Lisa: I think it appeared after the funeral but I wasn't really sure how long it had been there. So one night I told my parents I was going to bed early since I wasn't feeling well. I got to my room and lay down on my bed, watching it. About ten minutes later I heard some quiet rustling behind the door and a shadow move in front of it and it just stayed there.

Kelly: *Lord.*

Lisa: My heart started racing and I turned over on my side, pretending I didn't notice. I just stared at the wall, not knowing what to do and I felt like crying but I also felt like storming into the bathroom.

Kelly: I would've.

Lisa: I stared at the wall for I think like five minutes then turned back onto my back and looked at the hole and the shadow was still there. I couldn't help it, I just stared at the hole for a few seconds and then the shadow moved and I heard some quiet footsteps.

Kelly: I would have kicked his ass, I'm sorry but I just would have.

Lisa: I just got under my covers and remember that I started crying. I cried for a while before I fell asleep with my clothes on. I woke up the next morning and stayed in bed until my mom made me get up.

Kelly looks down at the floor, thinking.

Kelly: I'm sorry.

Lisa: I sat in the shower that morning for at least twenty minutes and it was then that it dawned on me that I didn't really know how long he'd been watching me. I mean I didn't. I could guess but I just wasn't sure.

She shifts her body and props up her head.

Lisa: I sat down in the shower just letting the water hit the back of my head and realized that for about the last year I had gotten in the habit of masturbating every night before I fell asleep. You know, I was just discovering it and it felt so good that I was experimenting with different ways, and I got to the point that I just couldn't fall asleep without doing it. And I never bothered to do it under the covers, always just on top of my bed. (*Then*) And when I realized this I started throwing up right where I sat in the tub.

And with this Kelly lights the weed, puts the tube to her lips and takes a long hit.

Lisa: I mean, I used a frickin' *carrot* once.

She places her hands over her face and starts laughing. So does Kelly.

Kelly: (*Points to herself*) Hairbrush.

Lisa: Highlighter.

Kelly: (*Nodding*) Lime green, for about a month.

Lisa laughs harder.

Kelly: Well, if it makes you feel any better, that *honestly* sounds like something my father would have the capacity to do.

She looks up quickly, pointing.

Kelly: I just lost the ceiling.

Lisa: I don't know *why* I told you all that.

Kelly: It's easier to tell strangers crap.

Lisa: I think it's how he dealt with the suicide.

Kelly: Odd fucking way to go about it.

Lisa: *Really.*

Kelly: Don't really see the connection.

The iPod changes to the next song.

And with this a Man wearing a three-piece suit stands up from the other side of the bed. He stands over Lisa and he's staring at the bed. He looks solemn.

Kelly sees this and braces her hands on the pillow

chair, sitting a bit more upright. She opens her mouth slightly as if to say something but nothing comes out.

Lisa: I don't either, but I tried to find some connection to make sense of it. I mean, I think my dad's a good guy, he's a pretty good father. Was always a good father--

The Man reaches down and stands back up with a shotgun in his hand. He wedges the shotgun into the baseboard of the bed so the barrel is pointing at the headboard.

Kelly manages to raise her arm and point to him.

Lisa: --maybe it was his way of trying to feel alive or young or something, as he faced death like that. (*Then realizing Kelly's pointing*) What?

Kelly: Look behind you.

Lisa: What?

The Man sits on the bed behind Lisa and simply looks down the barrel of the shotgun.

Kelly: (*Quietly*) *Behind* you.

Lisa turns onto her back and looks behind her.

Lisa: *What...*

She studies Lisa's reaction, confused.

The Man tightens his necktie and shuffles closer to the end of the barrel.

Kelly: Oh my God.

Lisa: What's the *matter?*

Kelly's frozen where she sits. She wants to move but can't.

The Man reaches for the trigger with the barrel just inches from his forehead.

Kelly closes her eyes and places her head in her hands and curls up into a fetal position.

Kelly: *No.*

And with this we hear footsteps climbing the stairs somewhere beyond the door of the bedroom. The Man gets up off the bed, removes the shotgun and disappears to the opposite side of the bed.

Kelly pops back up -- frantically looking at the bed. With The Man now gone, she looks at the door. The footsteps are getting louder.

Kelly: Shit.

Lisa starts to sit up. Kelly gets up, grabs a towel and starts fanning the air toward the open window. And as the footsteps get louder she starts for the door when…

The door opens and Sara enters holding a laundry basket.

Lisa: Thought that was locked.

She looks at Lisa then to Kelly then back to Lisa -- then sees the hookah.

Sara: Get downstairs *right now*. *And* your friend.

She leaves.

They simply stare at each other, not sure what to do. And with that we hear Sara yell from the hall…

Sara: (*O.S.*) Now!

Karma Canyon

Saturday, 7:30 PM

The kitchen / living room. Sara quickly descends the stairs, still carrying the laundry basket.

Sara: Art! Get in here please -- we need to talk.

She drops the laundry basket in the kitchen then walks to the island counter where she pours herself a glass of red wine.

Frank enters and sits at the counter.

Frank: What's wrong now?

Sara: Art!

She drinks.

Sara: This doesn't concern you.

Frank: Good.

Kelly and Lisa enter. Sara eyes Lisa.

Lisa: Look, I'm sorry about this.

Sara: Well, I think it's just best if you went home. I *could* call the police…I could.

Kelly: I don't think she should have to go anywhere.

Sara: Art!...Is he in the garage?

Taking her glass of wine, Sara walks across the living room and exits through a door stage left.

Frank: What the hell were you two doing up there?

Kelly: Shut up, Frank. (*Then*) I'm having a glass too.

She walks to the island and pours it. We hear Sara yelling for Art, offstage.

Frank: That should help the situation.

Lisa: (*To Kelly*) Maybe I should get going.

Kelly: You don't have to go anywhere; it'll blow over in about ten minutes because they won't really know how to handle this, which is interesting in itself, really.

She sits on a stool and offers one to Lisa.

Kelly: Just sit, *really*.

Hesitantly, she does.

Sara: (*O.S.*) Art! In the kitchen!

Sara enters stage left.

Frank: Were you guys making out or something?

Sara: Frank, go find something to do.

And with that Frank's cell phone rings. He flips it open and starts talking as he exits — passing by...

Art. He enters unknowingly, head down fumbling through a toolbox.

Kelly and Lisa turn to face him.

Art: (*Yelling to the unseen Sara*) I'm *in* the kitchen!

Lisa gets up off her stool and stands.

Sara: Where the hell've you been? I went around the house three times.

Art: Next door looking for an Allen wrench.

Art finally looks up from the toolbox toward Kelly and Lisa.

He stops.

Lisa stares back at him. Neither moves.

Kelly lowers her brow, looks at Lisa then to her father.

Kelly: You two know each other or something?

Sara looks at Art, then at Lisa, until...

Sara: Art, we need to have a sit-down with your daughter.

Art finally manages to put the tool box on the table. Nervously, he continues to dig through the various tools in the box. Kelly watches this, then looks at Lisa. Lisa still hasn't moved.

Sara: Art, did you hear me? Can you put the toolbox down for a second?

Art: (*Nervous*) Sara, let's save this for another time, huh? Whatever it is you need to talk about, I'm sure it can wait until we have a little family time, don't you think?

Kelly: I agree, it's really not that big a deal, but as usual, mom's overreacting to human nature.

Sara: Your daughter was smoking pot in her bedroom, in this house. I just caught her.

Kelly: Lisa gets it for medical purposes, so it's legal.

She looks to Lisa for backup but instead Lisa walks over to the couch and sits.

Sara: They were smoking it out of a pipe the size of a yardstick.

Kelly: It's a *hookah.*

Sara: I don't care what it's called, it's illegal and doing it under our roof is…*no way*, just no way--

Kelly gets up off the stool.

Sara: --and it puts us at risk, it's a crime. And what if the neighbors smell it?

Kelly: Not when it's for medical purposes.

Sara: There *are* no medical purposes, not for you!

Art: Sara. *Easy…*

Kelly: I've been having hallucinations, it helps temper them.

Sara: *No.* We don't have hallucinations, not *here*--

Kelly: (*Points upstairs*) I just saw a man with a shotgun sitting on my bed!

Art rubs his temples.

Sara: Well I think it's pretty obvious *why* you might

see a man in your bedroom--

Kelly: (*Puts her arms up*) Ok. See, we're going to go around like this for about an hour--

Sara: --I wasn't born yesterday.

Kelly: --around and around like mental patients, so I think I'll spare everyone the trouble.

She turns for the stairs.

Kelly: (*To Lisa*) You can come up if you want.

Sara: No, she can't...I'd prefer it if you went home and took your drugs with you, and I'll spare you a trip downtown.

Kelly: There *is* no downtown here. Part of the appeal, remember?

Lisa stands and places a hand on her stomach.

Lisa: I think I need to go to the bathroom.

She walks into the adjacent bathroom and closes the door.

Kelly: (*Yelling to the bathroom*) Come back up when you're done. You don't have to leave.

Kelly exits up the stairs.

Kelly: (O.S.) Not when it's for medical!

Art takes out two wrenches and measures them against each other. Sara walks closer to Art.

Sara: You haven't said anything. We always do this, we brush over things and nothing gets resolved.

Art: Sara, we're going to have to do this another time -- we'll get to it, we really will.

Sara: No, Art.

She tries to grab one of the wrenches; he quickly blocks her.

Art: Stop it.

Sara: Don't try to ignore the situation.

Art slams the wrenches into the toolbox with a crash of metal.

Art: (*Yelling*) Stop pushing me! *I said*, we'll talk about this another time.

He takes another tool out of the box but throws it back down with another crash.

She stares at him on the verge of tears.

He walks over to the island and grabs the bottle of wine.

Art: And the fucking drinking…

He pours the bottle of wine down the sink.

Art: The goddamned wine and the minute there's a crisis in this house. You wonder why your daughter thinks she can get away with murder...

He looks at her and exhales. She's crying. He places both hands on the counter, head down.

She takes a towel from the laundry basket and places it to her eyes.

A long silence before…

Sara: Who is that in the bathroom?

Art looks up at her slowly.

Art: I don't know.

She looks at him, wiping her eyes.

Sara: (*Quietly*) Oh…seems like that isn't the case.

And with that Sara turns and exists up the stairs.

Art closes his eyes and breathes in constant, slow breaths. He does this repeatedly until the bathroom door finally opens and Lisa appears. She's been crying. She looks about the room to notice everyone gone. Art stays behind the island. He grabs the corners of the counter with both hands.

He looks at her for a long moment until...

Art: Did you know I lived here?

Lisa: I wouldn't be here if I had.

Art: Right.

A silence.

Lisa: Patterson came to see me.

Art: I know.

Lisa: I can still press charges, you know that...I should press charges.

Art: I didn't do anything wrong, and you know that.

Lisa: The *minimum* sentence is five years.

Art: Why are you doing this to me?

Lisa: *Five.*

Nothing...

Lisa: Think about that. Everything you have would be gone.

He stands and takes a step toward her.

Art: If you think I have money and this is a way to get some, you're mistaken.

Lisa: It's my word against yours, I guess.

Art: You'd try to take advantage of an innocent person just because society may believe you? Well, let me tell you, you know I'm innocent and you don't have a case. If you want to go to court, then get ready for a counter-suit, and then you'll be in way over your head. Hope you have a few hundred thousand in the bank.

Lisa: *You* say you're innocent.

Art: You're just a kid....You know my heart was in it, to help you learn and you took advantage of that. For what, to get some type of settlement, make a little easy money and ruin a man's life in the process? (*Then*) Don't go out into the world that way, Lisa, I'm telling you now. You don't want to be that person.

Lisa: It would still just be your word against mine. Who would society believe...who would your neighbors believe?

Art: Probably you.

Lisa: *Right*.

He casually reaches into the toolbox and pulls out a screwdriver. He holds it up to the light like a knife before walking towards her slowly, closing in on her.

She stiffens.

Art: You have thirty seconds to get out of my house.

And with this she immediately steps back, turns, and exits the door stage left.

The door closes with a soft click.

Art walks back to the toolbox and places the screwdriver back in. He searches through the various tools until he pulls out the exact two wrenches from earlier. And as if they had never left his grasp, he holds one in each hand, placing them together in a methodical effort to compare and contrast them in the angles of light afforded by the kitchen's ceiling lamps.

He takes a towel and begins wiping them, slowly and with care.

The stage lights fade to black.

Beneath the Diamond Skies

12 Hours Earlier

Saturday, 7:22 AM

The Kitchen. Sara, in her bathrobe, descends the staircase. An early morning sun is just rising and shedding light through the window — affording the room a warm glow, a hopeful beginning to this day. She walks to the counter and begins to make a pot of coffee as Art descends the staircase, also in his bathrobe. He walks directly to the kitchen table and sits, opening a magazine.

Sara hits the button on the clock radio. Bob Dylan's "Mr. Tambourine Man" plays. Art looks up from his magazine for a moment, then returns to reading. Sara sits at the opposite end of the table and watches him read.

Sara: This song always made me sad.

Art: That's why it's one of your favorite songs.

Sara: Well, happy anniversary to you *too*.

He looks to her playfully.

Art: You too.

Sara: We have a lot to be thankful for.

He places his finger into the magazine to mark his spot and closes it.

Art: I got you something I think you're really going to like -- I can't give it to you now, we'll wait until we go out tonight. It'll be more fun.

Sara: Did you make reservations?

Art: The steak house, the table by the saltwater tank you like.

Sara: So much for surprises.

Art: You just *asked*.

Sara: I know, but….Coulda held out a *little* longer.

Art: We don't have to go…I thought you liked it there.

Sara: I'm sorry, just joking around.

Art: I know when you're joking, Sara.

Sara: You do?

Art: After twenty years, I think so.

Sara: Well sometimes it's just nice to be…(*Thinking*) Come here…I have something for you too.

Art: What is it?

Sara: Just come here.

Art: Is the coffee done?

She drops her shoulders, cocks her head.

Sara: It's a new tool box but I have it under the table, so you'll have to come get it.

He walks to the window and pulls down the shade…

Sara: What are you doing?

…then sits back down at the table opposite her.

Art: You want the neighbors to see us?

She pushes her chair back and begins to crawl under the table.

She crawls towards him in a way that would suggest a forced sensuality, a disjointed slither, closer, closer until she places her head between his thighs, disappearing under his blue terrycloth robe.

He looks at the coffee pot. We hear various unintelligible mumblings under the robe and then silence as the robe raises and lowers in a calculated rhythm. Art's stare moves from the coffee pot to the table in front of him, almost without expression. "Yesterday" by Paul McCartney begins to play on the radio. He picks up the radio remote, points it towards the radio, and increases the volume.

He reaches for the magazine but then thinks better of it and leaves it be, deciding to simply lean back.

And this goes on until Kelly descends the staircase, sleepily, in her sweatpants and tank top. She enters the kitchen and stops mid-stride at the scene before her. Art, in his pleasure-haze, slowly turns and looks at her. His expression doesn't change, his robe rising and falling rhythmically to the sounds of McCartney.

Their eyes lock.

Kelly's mouth opens slowly as she cocks her head, looking under the table. Keeping eye contact, Art begins to breathe heavier, and heavier, until finally he closes his eyes. He holds his breath for a moment before finally grabbing Sara's blue terrycloth head, motioning for her to stop. Kelly turns and retreats back up the stairs. Sara emerges from under the robe, crawls back to her side of the table and surfaces again, hair tangled.

Sara: *That's* a happy anniversary….Kinda nice under there; maybe you should try it.

She slides down in her chair, spreads her legs slightly. He looks to her, then to the counter.

Art: Little coffee first.

He gets up and kisses her on the forehead.

Art*:* It felt great though, Sara.

She slides back up in her chair, crossing her legs and pulling the robe tightly around her thighs.

Sara: Well, I'm glad I can help you out.

Art: What car do you think we should take?

She takes a magazine from the table and opens it to a page, any page.

Sara: I don't know, Art -- I guess whichever one you want…the Corolla gets better mileage.

Art: It's our anniversary Sara…I think we can splurge a bit and take the other car. We should get the crème bruleé you like, with the espresso drinks, too.

Sara: I think we should take the kids with us tonight.

Art: Tonight?

Sara: I think we should -- I'd like to have the kids with us.

Art: Well, if you want to…

He fills his cup and opens the shade. She notices this, then looks back down at her magazine.

Sara: It should be about the kids anyway, today I mean, in addition to us. I just think it's got to be about more than just us--

She turns the page.

Sara: --it's just got to be.

Art: Well, if you want to, that's fine, but I thought today would be about us.

He sits back down.

Sara: I thought today we could go see the exhibit I've been wanting to see, in the city.

Art: Today? Oh, I forgot to tell you, I have a session today with a student.

Sara: With whom?

Art: Brad, he's a first year student.

She closes the magazine quickly.

Sara: Oh…again?

Art: He's been having some trouble.

Sara: Where's the session?

Art: He's coming here.

Sara: *Here*? Why?

Art: I guess just a change.

Sara: Whose idea was *that*?

Art: What does it matter where?

Sara: What's wrong with campus?

Art: *Nothing*, what the hell does it matter where?

Sara: How many times have you met him in the last month?

Art: I don't know. A few. I meet with a lot of students.

Sara: So you suggested he come to our *house*.

Art: I don't know.

Sara: You don't know…

Art: I thought --

Sara: He certainly didn't invite *himself* over.

Art: --I thought it would be a friendly environment, a nice change from the faculty building.

Sara: A nice change for you two.

He looks at her quickly.

Art: What are you trying to *say*?

Sara: I'm not trying to *say* anything…I just think our home should be for us, not for *sessions*.

Art: Well I'm sorry you feel that way and with the anniversary and everything, but he's coming over today.

She opens the magazine again and pages through it faster -- forward, then backward.

Sara: Well, what *time* is he coming? I wish you would have told me about this.

Art: If this is about scheduling things for our anniversary, then I'm sorry. I said we're doing the steakhouse at nine, and I'm sorry it wasn't a surprise.

He looks down to his lap.

Art: I hate this robe.

Sara: I just always want us to be truthful with each other. If we don't have that, we don't have anything.

Art: I thought we *were*…What does that have to do with being truthful? (*Then*) You're the one trying to say something -- what are you trying to say?

Sara: You don't hate your robe.

Art: *Yes.* I do hate my robe. It makes me feel old. Terrycloth makes me feel old. Young guys don't wear terrycloth *anything.*

Sara: I just would like to hear you say you love me… more often.

Art: I do.

Sara: See?

She gets up and walks to the island, a pause…

He looks at her and leans forward, placing his elbows on the table.

Art: We've created a good home, Sara. A normal home for our kids, and I like to think we've done a good job…with Kelly and Frank, they're good kids. Not all our friends can say that….We have what we always said we wanted.

Sara: I know that.

Art: Then what is it, Sara? What more do you want?

She walks to the refrigerator.

Sara: Frank's in college soon. I just can't bear to think of this house without the kids here.

Art: It's what kids *do,* Sara -- they leave.

Sara: I want to know there's something in our future when the kids are gone, something that's different, you know, the next phase of our lives…it's just … something important to think about.

Art: What we have *is* our future.

She looks to him.

Art: Come on, Sara…if you're talking about a couple of trips or new cruise lines, you know, of course, that's never been a problem. I love those things. I'm still going to get all the faculty discounts, but it's a bit of a pipe dream to think our lives are going to change dramatically in the next thirty years. *(He exhales)*…Jesus, Sara -- we have *fifteen* years left on the mortgage.

She begins to wipe the counter with a rag.

Art: That counter is already *clean.*

Sara: I'd really like Frank to go to school here next year -- I really would.

Art: That's a dead horse, he wants to go to New York…or abroad…*you're* the one who planted that in his head. Now it's not a good idea? What about the big speech that you never took advantage of the opportunity so he should and experience the world when he's young -- Vienna, was it?…Don't do that to him.

He gets up and opens the refrigerator.

Sara: (*Quietly*) I'm just afraid I'm going to get to the point where I can't bear this neighborhood anymore.

Art stops. He stares at the contents of the refrigerator, simply holding the door.

Kelly descends the staircase.

Art: I'm afraid you've already gotten to that point, Sara.

Kelly enters.

Kelly: What *point* have you gotten to?

Startled, Art turns to see Kelly right behind him.

Art: Sneaking up on people now?

Sara: Hi honey, how'd you sleep?

Art sits back down at the table, returning to his magazine. Kelly pours a cup of coffee.

Kelly: Dad said you've already "gotten to that point."

Sara: It's nothing, really, just talking some things through.

Kelly sits down opposite Art and looks at him.

Kelly: Hi, Daddy.

Art: (*Cautious*) Hi, sweetie.

Kelly: So…how has *your* morning been?

Art: (*Quickly*) Your mom and I were just talking some things through.

Sara walks to Kelly and kisses her on the head.

Sara: How much we love you kids. You're up early, sweetie.

Kelly: (*Staring at Art*) Yeah, I guess so. You know, it's strange, I came down earlier —

Art: *Kelly…*

She stops and looks at him, cocking her head.

Kelly: Yes?

Art: Where's your brother, still sleeping?

Kelly: Probably pumping himself.

Sara: He does *not*.

Kelly: That's *all* he does.

Frank descends the stairway.

Art: He's a busy kid, lay off him.

Frank enters.

Frank: What's goin' on?

Kelly spins around.

Kelly: We were just talking about how much you love yourself when you're in your bedroom.

He turns right back around and exits, disappearing back up the staircase.

Sara: (*To Frank*) Honey! Come back down, she didn't mean that!

Kelly: (*To Frank*) Yes, I did! (*Then*) It's just, a little strange behavior is all...I mean, don't you think, Art?

Art: Maybe you'd like a little breakfast and stop worrying about your brother so much -- he can take care of himself.

Kelly: *Obviously.*

Sara: He's perfectly normal.

Kelly: Oh really? And how do we define *normal* in this household?

Sara inhales...

Sara: How about some decaf sweetie.

Kelly: Decaf's a joke.

Art: I think you're prying for trouble is what I think. Can you give us a little break here for once?

Kelly retracts, looks at him for a moment, then gets up and heads for the coffee pot again.

Kelly: It's just that it's a bit traumatic when you come downstairs and see your father getting a blowjob at seven in the morning.

Sara drops a plate.

Art looks down to the table. Sara looks at Kelly. Kelly looks at Art.

Kelly pours herself a cup of coffee.

Kelly: You see, it's not the *blowjob* that bothers me so much--

Kelly is now staring at Art who refuses to look back.

Kelly: --It's the fact that he saw me…and did…absolutely…nothing about it.

They are now both staring at him.

Kelly: Instead, he decided it was somehow better to let me watch.

Art slowly turns the page of the magazine. Finally, Kelly turns, walks across the stage and exits.

Sara's staring at him. He turns another page.

Sara: *What* is the matter with you?

He gets up and walks to the cupboard, opening it.

Art: She makes it sound *very* negative.

He looks in the cupboard, closes it, then walks to her, placing his hand around her waist.

Art: You know how dramatic she is. (*He manages a slight smirk*)…Honey, I was seriously at the point of…you know. When she walked in. What was I supposed to do?…Point of no return.

He kisses her on the forehead.

Art: Kelly's about drama, we know that. She exaggerates.

They look at each other…

She turns from him and begins to start breakfast.

Sara: Let's just get this going…I'm hungry.

Art: Me too.

Sara: I'll talk to her later.

And with this they begin the simple ritual they've done so many times before. But this time in silence. They cross back and forth. A cupboard opening. Closing. The beating of eggs in a dish. Bread from the freezer. The microwave door opening, closing. This continues in an awkward silence until...

Art: We have a good life, Sara...

She says nothing. He places slices of bread into the toaster.

Art: We have each other to come home to at night... we have *stability*. And our *kids*, that gives us purpose, *that* if anything should give us a future.

He opens a cupboard, retrieves four plates and places them on the island. He then goes back up to the cupboard and pulls down four glasses and places them next to the dishes. He's waiting for a response, but gets nothing.

Art: If you're not happy Sara, if you're not happy with me or yourself, you have choices, we all have choices in our lives. If it's wanting to make your life better for you, to get out of this neighborhood where the houses drive you insane, for some experience you never got because you still wonder every night when you go to bed what you would've become had you lived in Vienna, who you would've met...

Sara: That's not fair.

Art: But it's the truth. You've known it for a long time…and I know it…But you know what? I have truths too, Sara, but I've learned to accept them. And the reality is, is that this *is* our life and it's best to accept it, for the good and the bad.

Again, he waits for a response, but she offers nothing.

Art: When the days roll into each other, week after week, you don't think I have feelings that living this life is essentially *enduring*? That I don't feel the need to create circumstances to feed *my* interest, just to feel alive? Jesus, Sara, it's a responsibility I have to myself.

She continues about her work, not looking at him. He wipes his hands on the towel and places it on the island counter.

Art: You're not the only one, Sara. I'm sorry to say this, but you're not unique. Not in this household, not in the house next door. Not in the house next to that one…(*Then*)…But it doesn't change the fact that I'm in love with you. Because really I come home every night and am still amazed by your eyes. You probably don't know that…because I guess I don't tell you anymore. Because life's gotten in the way… but I've always been...

He picks up his coffee cup and looks into it.

Art: --*you're* why I want to survive all this.

He hesitates, waiting…nothing…

He places his cup back down.

Art: I'm going to take a shower…before we all eat.

The toast pops up like a gunshot. They both ignore it.

Another silence until…

Art: You're not the only one who drives down this street every day and is devastated by the thought that we're trying to live important, interesting lives among all this.

Sara: It's not going to keep me from trying.

Art: Our life together shouldn't keep either of us from trying, ever…(*Then*) I think we're at the point where we just have to take it day by day.

He turns to leave.

Art: Starting with this one…

And with this he walks across the kitchen, exits, and disappears up the stairs.

Sara stands alone for a long moment, thinking. She walks to the window and looks at her ghost-like reflection in the window pane. She combs through her hair with her fingers, adjusting.

TIMOTHY HARSH

She quietly turns to the pieces of toast which have already hardened from neglect. She opens the trash can and throws them in before placing two new slices in the toaster. Then pulling two handfuls of silverware from the drawer, she begins setting the table. She moves methodically about each setting, ensuring each of the four spots are equally and properly represented with the following matching ware: a turquoise plate; a dark blue cloth napkin; a five-inch tall juice glass; and the following in brushed, stainless steel, placed in order from left to right: a fork, a butter knife, a spoon.

Stage lights fade to black.

End.

Epilogue

Suburbia. It always struck me as an interesting setting for a story. Through the eastern slopes of the Rocky Mountains outside of Denver, along the Great Salt Lake in Utah on the approach to Salt Lake City, the endless urban sprawl on the outskirts of Los Angeles, through the eastern suburban tracts of The Bay Area; Livermore, Pleasanton, as one drives west to San Francisco. In each case, what always strikes me are the planned tracts of model houses in various tones of tan, packed neatly together, strung along hillsides, curving in upon themselves and often times into an increasingly brownish air until the last few houses in the string disappear into something that exists only if you're living in it. Probably four or five hundred at a glance, each with its measured patch of green grass in the front and back. And for variety, a small sapling with the little black rubber ring imprisoning the circle of wood chips supporting its skinny trunk. The rows upon rows of these houses appear so lifeless from the road, yet I know each harbors the opposite, each has been erected to offer a comfortable, safe, middle-American setting for its occupants. The genius of predetermining the demand of a safety net for our middle-class. Something this well thought-out and free from inaccuracies should harbor good, normal, happy lives where soccer balls and spa coupons seep from open windows. At the very least, each house has a story, is what I think every time I drive past these neighborhoods. From the freeway they appear so quiet, unmoving and calm as if each one is deserted. As I drive by sometimes I pick out one house in the exact middle of the longest row and think about its occupants, their story. Certainly they have one. Certainly it's a story worth telling. I divert my attention from the house momentarily and see the exit sign approaching: green with the name of the overpass street in reflective lettering and an arrow pointing towards the house — This way to Middle America. This way to our dreams. This way to what you've worked so hard for. This way to fit in. And as I approach the sign I think about slowing down and pulling off to find out the story, what's going on behind all the rows of stucco and tile, full of secrets. Maybe their lives are interesting. Maybe they're not. Who knows. But I do know this: something's going on in all those well-behaved houses. And I want to know the good parts, and I really want to know the bad parts. There's got to be bad parts because the well behaved "how are ya's" with logo-littered tennis shorts screams debauchery within. "Tragedy-Light," a modified tragedy, but only on the surface, a surface that needs to be maintained like the lawns because a Dodge Caravan is best driven on a full tank with perfect tire pressure. And on the lawn, I don't know why, but a perfectly kept lawn always struck me as a cover for something, a longing, a cover-combatant to slight malaise, if not outright depression. And about the time that thought enters my mind is when I inevitably come upon the exit and decide to keep driving. I guess because I don't want to be disappointed at the least, or intimidated at the most, by the reality of it all. It's safer to invent it. So as the sign flashes by I give the family one last encouraging thought for a happy life filled with interesting moments and a bit of sitcom-chaos to fight the inevitable routine of fighting routine. And I keep going because there's really no time to dwell too much on this tract, there'll be another one up the road. There always is.

-Timothy Harsh
San Francisco
February 2003

Breinigsville, PA USA
06 January 2011
252811BV00001B/6/P